THE RIOTOUS PASSIONS OF ROBBIE BURNS

Robert Burns

THE RIOTOUS PASSIONS OF ROBBIE BURNS

The Imaginative Retelling of a True Story

JOHN IVISON

Ottawa Press and Publishing

ISBN (softcover) 978-1-988437-55-2
ISBN (epub) 978-1-988437-57-6
ISBN (mobi) 978-1-988437-56-9

Cover, design, composition:
Magdalene Carson / New Leaf Publication Design

Published in Canada

Library and Archives Canada Cataloguing in Publication

Title: The riotous passions of Robbie Burns : the imaginative retelling of a true story / John Ivison.
Names: Ivison, John, author.
Identifiers: Canadiana (print) 20200379275 | Canadiana (ebook) 20200379364 | ISBN 9781988437552 (softcover) | ISBN 9781988437576 (EPUB) | ISBN 9781988437569 (Kindle)
Subjects: LCSH: Burns, Robert, 1759-1796—Fiction.
Classification: LCC PS8617.V57 R56 2020 | DDC C813/.6—dc23

James, Fiona and William
— exiled sons and daughter of Scotland

"Far have you wandered over seas of longing,
And now you drowse, and now you well may weep,
When all the recollections come a-thronging
Of this rude country where your fathers sleep."

"To Exiles," Neil Munro

TABLE OF CONTENTS

To the Reader

This book was born from frustration. As Scotland's other national poet Hugh MacDiarmid wrote, Robert Burns is revered, yet "no' wan in 50 kens a wurd (he) wrote." The church of Burns has debased his brilliance with suppers, paperweights and tea-towels.

Using Burns' own letters as the basis for his dialogue, this work of fiction was aimed at bringing this fascinating character back to life, as he struggled to love and prosper in a world where the odds were stacked against someone from his background.

Thanks to Ron Corbett of Ottawa Press and Publishing for buying into that vision; to Magdalene Carson for the design and cover illustration; and Bernadette Cox for such a thorough copy-editing. All mistakes are my own.

Love and gratitude also to my wife, Dana, for her constant support and advice. I'm glad she never met Rabbie.

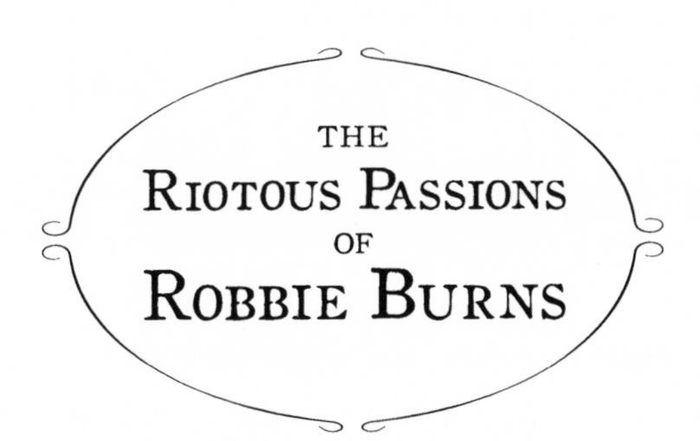
THE
RIOTOUS PASSIONS
OF
ROBBIE BURNS

CHAPTER I

From the distance of nearly three decades, I can reminisce about Burns with great fondness. He took me under his wing, taught me how to bend Cupid's bow and held me in the grip of his charming sorcery. He was a bewitching figure—someone once said of him that when you shook hands, it was as if he burnt you.

Yet there were occasions where he behaved damnably and persuaded me to be complicit in many of his deceits. His belief that poets should be governed by different rules of conduct than everyone else inflicted scars that took many years to heal.

It was scarcely surprising that the man inspired mixed emotions—he was a mass of contradictions: capable of beauty and baseness, sensitive to the promise of life but also its many pitfalls, gifted with confidence and accomplishment while crippled with self-doubt. He possessed a rare kindness but cruelty, too. Being in his orbit was exhilarating and exhausting.

The night we met was a typical grey Edinburgh evening. I wandered into Johnnie Dowie's tavern and headed to the narrow little room at the back, ominously named "The Coffin." I looked in to see Richmond, Nicol and a third man—part peasant, part dandy—clad in a coat the russet brown colour of dead leaves, his brown hair tied back in a way that was not yet fashionable and with no trace of powder. He had eyes that were clear and strong and probing. The group sat eating oysters and drinking porter while the stranger held court. My friends did not see me, so I let him continue with his story before entering.

"We ranged around a bowl until the good-fellow hour of six and then went out to pay our devotions to the glorious lamp of day," he said. "We saddled up and spent the day passing the bottle as we rode. But then a Highlandman came past us at a gallop on a tolerably good horse that had never known the ornament of iron or leather. We scorned to be out-galloped by a Highlandman, so off we started, whip and spur. My companions fell astern, but my old mare was not called Rocinante for naught. She was as fleet as Don Quixote's horse and strained past the Highlandman in spite of all his efforts with the hair halter. Just as I was passing, Donald wheeled his horse, as if to cross before me to mar my progress. But ere he could, down came his horse and threw his rider's breeckless arse into a hedge. Then down came Rocinante and my bardship between her and the Highlandman's horse. Neither horses nor riders came off as badly as might have been expected—just a few cuts and bruises and a thorough resolution to be the pattern of sobriety in the future." With that he raised his bumper and winked at me as the others howled in laughter.

I entered somewhat red of face for having eaves-dropped, but I need not have worried. When Richmond and Nicol saw me, they rose and ushered me to take a seat.

"Rab, this is the newest recruit to our band of revelry, John Bruce. John, meet the poet laureate and bard-in-chief over the districts and counties of Kyle, Cunningham and Carrick, Robert Burns."

"Too kind, too kind, sir. Mr. Bruce come and join us for some homely fare," the man introduced as Robert Burns said to me.

"Mr. Burns, pleased to make your acquaintance," I said back. "I'd heard you were bound for Jamaica?"

"Well my chest of belongings was already on the road to a ship harboured in Greenock when I received word that Dr. Thomas Blacklock, the esteemed blind poet and scholar, held my Kilmarnock Edition in some regard, and that roused my poetic ambition. His idea that I would meet with every encouragement in the capital for a second edition fired me so much that I posted to Edinburgh without a single acquaintance, bar our mutal friend, John Richmond, and not a single letter of introduction in my pocket."

"So what's next for you?" I asked.

"What's next, my boy, is a trip to Dawnie Douglas' tavern to introduce Mr. Burns to the Crochallan Fencibles," interrupted Nicol.

I'd heard about this club, ostensibly a band of citizens formed as 'fencible men' or volunteers against the dangers arising from invasion. But this was no ordinary fencible club. It was a social gathering, with mock military pretensions, of some of Edinburgh's most eminent citizens, named after an old Gaelic song the proprietor was in the habit of singing to his guests—The Cattle of Colin or Chro challin.

When the happy triumvirate I had joined had finished eating and drinking, we made our way to a neighbouring close, where a sign read "Anchor Tavern Howff," with a scale stair leading down.

We descended and found a group of men arranged around a long table with three older gentlemen at the head. Nicol was hailed on his entrance to the Crown Room at the back of the tavern by the foremost man, who seemed to be in charge. He returned the greeting. "Colonel Dunbar," said Nicol, "I have brought you two new recruits, including the poet whose star is blazing across our skies, Mr. Robert Burns. Jock Richmond I think you have met, and may I present my kinsman from Annandale, John Bruce."

"Gentlemen, come in and take a seat. Welcome to the Crochallan Fencibles, a body of men who can scarcely discern between right hand or left for drunkenness. "I'm William Dunbar, WS. Our military rank is as ludicrous as the threat to our security from the Americas. But we like to add a degree of formality to our revels. To my left is Mr. Charles Hay, our muster-master general, who is charged with drilling the recruits. To my right is our esteemed founder and sergeant-at-arms, Mr. William Smellie," he said, pointing to a man in mid-life who, having apparently grown careless of his costume and appearance, had a shabby coat, grisly growth on his chin and uncombed locks.

"You will meet the other members in due course: Mr. Cleghorn, Mr. Cunningham, Mr. Johnson, Mr. Masterton, Mr. Hill and Mr. Gordon. But a question first, Mr. Burns—are you a lover of the ladies?"

Burns stepped forward into the light and thought for a minute. "Sir, I am the greatest fool when woman is the presiding star. So much so that I am honouring my king by begetting him loyal subjects," he said to a murmur of general satisfaction from the membership.

"Well said, sir," replied Dunbar. "Then you will join us in saving the ladies. The rules to the game are simple. Each man has to propose his own girl as the loveliest of her sex, drink to her glory and vow to die in her defence. The one who drinks most and falls prone last is the victor."

At this point bumpers were raised, toasts made and Smellie rose unsteadily to his feet before launching into a chorus:

"Come rede me, dame, come tell me, dame,
My dame come tell me truly,
What length o' graith, when weel ca'd hame,
Will sair a woman duly?
The carlin clew her wanton tail,
Her wanton tail sae ready,
I learn'd a sang in Annandale
Nine inch will please a lady."

The Crochallan Fencibles had been called to arms.

CHAPTER II

My days had begun to take on a predictable minuet, consisting of my emergence from my chamber in a crapulous state after a night at Johnnie Dowie's tavern, a draft of ale at breakfast to dull damaged nerve ends and then a day of settling accounts and conveyancing at the office of Samuel Mitchelson, WS. However, Burns and the Crochallan Fencibles were all in my future when I arrived in the capital in the late autumn, year of our Lord 1786, to take up an apprenticeship in law.

The old town seen for the first time was like a scene from one of those epic, ancient stories of endless battles and unhappy loves. As I rode in from the south, the naked, jagged rock of the castle appeared through the squalls of greasy sleet like something from Dante's Inferno. The city's gates rose up, as if they were the gates of Hell itself. Abandon all hope, ye who enter here, they seemed to say.

But for all its dark foreboding, it also suggested mystery and wild promise.

It was my first time in Edinburgh. It was my first time anywhere outside my native Annandale. It was already dark when I reached the Royal Mile in late afternoon. The sleet swirled, blowing into my face whichever direction I rode. The miserable residents, hunched and huddled under their hoods, sped as quickly as their legs could carry them into closes and wynds to escape the weather.

This was the fabled seat of the Scottish Enlightenment—a city that had not 90 years earlier hung a student for blasphemy after referring to the New Testament as the "history of the imposter Christ."

It had been a wild place. Only 40 years prior Captain John Porteous had been dragged from the Tolbooth and hanged by a mob for having ordered his soldiers to fire on an unruly crowd at a public execution. His body was hacked while he dangled. But the more genteel citizens had since then resolved to put the town's violent past behind it.

The battle for the soul of the country, between knowledge revealed by scripture and knowledge acquired by skepticism, had been fought and in large part won by thinkers like David Hume and Adam Smith. It was a realm of progress, governed by the light of reason.

Yet there was nothing welcoming or enlightened about the capital on this raw, late October afternoon. I was chilled to the marrow. The thought of living on this windswept crag, so far away from all I'd ever known, while I studied as a pupil at Samuel Mitchelson's law office, filled me with dread.

The castle, built on top of a great volcanic plug towering over the Royal Mile, appeared again briefly through the blizzard. The esplanade ran down from the crag—a tail connecting the castle to the High Street, with closes and wynds splintering off left and right.

If Auld Reekie had changed in recent years, so had the rest of Scotland. My family, the Bruces, had worked for generations as the stewards for the Johnstones, lairds of Galabank, in Annandale, abutting the border with England. My grandfather happened to be in the Queensberry Arms in Annan just as Charles Edward Stuart's army was retreating in disarray from its abortive attempt to place his line back on the throne. Some Highlanders were in the tavern, and when they heard my grandfather express his staunch adherence to the House of Hanover, they arrested him and took him to Glasgow with them. He asked to be interviewed by the Young Pretender himself, and when his wish was granted, he told the Prince the circumstance of his arrest.

"Sir, I commend you," said Charles. "If some of my pretended followers had been so firm in my cause as you are to George, I should now be on the throne of my fathers." Then he set him free—or so the story goes.

Since the failure of the Jacobite rebellion, it was widely considered a good idea to forget the past and shed any trappings of Scotland's proud and independent history. Fortunes were to be made by being more English than the English, not harking on about my ancient and distant ancestor, Robert the Bruce, the 8th Lord of Annandale, whose struggle for independence culminated in the Battle of Bannockburn in 1314. That old story about him watching a spider continually swinging from one wall to another to build its web, with its lessons about perseverance, was like an old hat. The modern way was to try and try and then give up. "Be happy living, for you're a long time dead" was the refrain in those days of peace and plenty.

Which suited me just fine. I'd dreamt of the revels of the capital since I was old enough to admire the Lord's workmanship in creating the fairer sex. I had a strong appetite for sociability that the small town of Annan could never satisfy. Yet the dream had become real, and every artery ran cold.

I had arranged for lodgings in Baxter's Close in the Lawnmarket, just below the castle, in the home of a widow called Mrs. Carfrae. After stabling my borrowed pony in the Grassmarket, I wandered up the High Street, marvelling at buildings six, seven, eight storeys high that seemed to scrape the heavens. Since there was only so much room to build inside Edinburgh's town walls, the solution seemed to be to build up and ever up. I rapped on the door of the address I'd been given, which was answered by a matronly, plainly dressed, hard-looking woman.

"Mrs. Carfrae? I'm John Bruce. I think you were expecting me?" I asked hopefully.

"Aye, I was. You're late," she said curtly as she ushered me in.

I spluttered an excuse about an ill wind blowing nobody any good, but she was obviously more used to talking than listening.

With no further fanfare, she led me through a room and kitchen as spartan as she was, up a narrow set of stairs and into a room with a sanded floor, a small table and a chaff bed.

"It'll be eighteenpence a week, and mind you pay on time or you'll be shown the door."

Warming to her sermon, she added, "I'll trust you will display good Christian virtues while you are under this roof. My late husband and I were very happy practicing good Christian virtues, but since he's gone this close has descended into skulduggery and sin. There are now a number of base jades, who lie with filthy fellows, drinking and singing abominable songs. They shall one day lie in Hell, weeping and wailing and gnashing their teeth over a cup of God's wrath. My husband, may he rest in peace, will be turning in his grave." With that, she gave a pious sniff and clacked off back down the stairs.

There would be no resting in peace for anyone in this house, I judged, collapsing on the bed. And not for the late and clearly lamented former master either, once his dear wife joined him in the Hereafter.

I was exhausted by eight hours in the saddle but also famished, having eaten the meagre bag of oatcakes and cheese I'd been carrying many hours earlier. Hunger drove me from the bed that was calling me into conference with the lumpy pillow. As I pulled the door to, I heard footsteps coming up the stairs. Not wishing to provoke the wrath of Mrs. Carfrae, I ducked back into my room, emerging in time to see the back of a tall man head down the hallway and turn into another room. I then tried to leave the house with some stealth but was caught in the act by Mrs. Carfrae who appeared to have been lying in wait.

"There'll be bannocks, porridge and crowdie at seven in the morning sharp. If you miss it, there'll be no food for you," she said.

"Erm…thank you. Very kind. Do you have other lodgers staying?" I ventured, trying to engage her softer side, only to find she didn't have one.

"Oh him. Mr. Richmond. He's another young law student. I have my doubts that he is an observant Christian. I suspect, more likely, that he is ungodly, enjoying the good things in life. He is even said to frequent that den of iniquity known as Johnnie Dowie's tavern down Libberton's Wynd. He is a sore and wicked tribulation," she lamented.

He sounded exactly the kind of fellow whose acquaintance I should be cultivating, I thought.

"Oh, I've just forgotten something in my room—my hat, yes my hat," I said excitedly.

"Your hat is on your head, you coof," she remonstrated.

"My other hat," I shouted over my shoulder, mounting the stairs in threes.

I walked along the hallway and knocked gently on the door of the man who must have been Mr. Richmond.

"Yes, can I help you, sir?" said a tall, elbow-faced lad of about my own age and height. He was dressed much as I was—in a drab, russet-coloured long tailcoat that looked as if it was worn constantly and had thus seen better days—corduroy breeches, a pale waistcoat and calf-length leather boots.

"Mr. Richmond, my name is Bruce, John Bruce, and I have just arrived from Annandale to apprentice at Samuel Mitchelson's law firm in Carrubber's Close. I am half-starved and fully parched. Mrs. Carfrae was kind enough to mention that you might know where I could best cure what ails me"

He stepped back, inspected me from head to foot and burst out laughing. "John Richmond. I'm a clerk with William Wilson, WS. Pleased to make your acquaintance. And call me Jock. Everyone else does," he said, extending his hand.

"Mrs. Carfrae is a good, pious Christian woman, whose main fault is she is lonely and misses her departed bedfellow. But she is sorely vexed at my mischievous nature, and I'm sure she didn't recommend you associate with my likes. But I will be avenged of her slander by taking you to the very spot where body and soul can best be reacquainted. Let me get my hat."

CHAPTER III

By the time we emerged from Baxter's Close, the sleet had abated, leaving a thick, oozing slush to cover our boots as we walked.

Richmond pointed to a house on the north side of the Lawnmarket. "That's where David Hume was born. He died in this city 10 years ago, and on his deathbed is said to have joked he wanted to negotiate a few more years of life with Charon, the ferryman of Hades, in order to witness 'the downfall of some of the prevailing systems of superstition'. He said he was told by the ferryman, 'You loitering rogue, that will not happen these many hundred years. Do you fancy I will grant you a lease for so long a term? Get into the boat this instant, you lazy loitering rogue.' But it is happening, and no one did more to change the old ways than Hume."

Richmond said he'd arrived in Edinburgh from Mauchline in Ayrshire to apprentice in law. "I was in flight from the holy beagles of the houghmagandie pack," he said, using the old Scots word for fornication, alluding to the public penance he'd been forced to endure after fathering a child out of wedlock.

We turned off the Lawnmarket, down Libberton's Wynd, only five feet wide, with buildings towering seven storeys high to left and right. Even on a night of terrible weather, such was the teeming mass of humanity sheltered within the buildings that people seeking space and solitude were sitting on the steps and stairwells. Halfway down the wynd, there was a painted sign proclaiming Johnnie Dowie's tavern. Richmond pulled on the door, and we walked into a scene from the festival of Bacchus, where wine, freedom, intoxication and ecstasy flowed without restraint. Through the smoke drifted laughter, both male and female, singing and a fiddle tune that sounded like a distillery set to music.

Behind a bar stood a round, pawky gentleman with a nose the colour of vintage port. "Come away in, gentlemen, there's corn in Egypt yet," hailed the landlord, whose establishment I would forever associate with conviviality.

After procuring a jug of claret, Richmond led us to a table away from the throng. There, a dishevelled looking character of some 40 or so years was snoring away like a Hessian.

"Brother Nicol. To arms, I've got someone I'd like you to meet," said Richmond.

The drink-palsied figure lifted his head and cursed. He was slovenly, though respectably dressed in a bottle green jacket and waistcoat. His face was bloated, and mottled flesh gathered under his chin. His hair was retreating toward his crown, like the tide going out.

"Saints preserve us, I've seen healthier faces peering from a coffin. Here, have a bumper of claret and you'll feel the benefit," said Richmond, pouring the wine. "John Bruce, meet William Nicol, classics master at the High School of Edinburgh and, if I'm not mistaken, a countryman of yours."

The wine appeared to be having a restorative effect on Nicol, who gulped it back in one and immediately demanded another. "Ye cannae drink the water in this place—it'll kill you, so there's nothing for it to slake your thirst but to drink pints of wine," he said by way of explanation.

Once he'd seen off another bumper, he turned to me. "So young Richmond here says we're countrymen. What's your story, boy?"

"Well, I've just arrived from Annandale to apprentice with Samuel Mitchelson, but I hail from near Annan where my family are stewards to the Laird of Galabank."

"Annan, eh? Did you go to the grammar school?

"That I did, sir."

"Well so did I, probably 20 years before you, mind. You're not related to old Jamie Bruce that took the Young Pretender to task for stealing the shoes off the people of Annandale on his route back north?"

"That was my grandfather, sir."

"Well, I'm not sure I share his conviction in the adequacies of the House of Hanover—an idiot race if ever there was one—but I admire his pluck. My father was a tailor in Ecclefechan, and I was born and educated in the royal burgh of Annan before coming to Edinburgh to attend the university."

Nicol appeared quite sober now and held forth on the subject of striking his pupils like gongs at regular intervals to instill the necessary discipline.

"I am accused of harshness toward the perverse dunces in my care. What the blockheaded parents cannot comprehend is that the skulls of the boobies they have for sons are impervious to science by any other means than fracture with a cudgel," he said as he raised yet another bumper. "Confusion to our enemies," he toasted.

Richmond and I slammed our glasses together as the music grew faster and more furious, as skirts were hitched higher while their occupants lounged on laps, as the laughter grew more raucous, as the room began to carousel out of control. And that's the last I remember before waking up in darkness, fully clothed, in my own bed. I woke to hear the bells of St. Giles sounding out seven times. I arranged myself as best I could and headed downstairs to find some water to bathe my blistering head. I found Richmond, grinning at me and tucking into a bowl of porridge. Around him, Mrs. Carfrae was clucking away like an old hen.

"Those daughters of the Devil. I tossed and turned, sleepless and looking for rest but finding none, thanks to the sinners living above. They will be roasted in Hell like herrings," she said before taking her leave.

Richmond chuckled. "She's just jealous that our night-rejoicing neighbours are revelling in vice while she has to lie awake on her own, listening to every squeak of the bedpost because the floors are so low and badly plastered. So how now, Mr. Bruce? You look like you are hanging by a thread."

"I fear my first day with the venerable law firm of Samuel Mitchelson is going to be very long indeed, thanks to your friend Mr. Nicol," I said, slumping down beside him.

"Well, at least you have some recollection of meeting him. I was obliged to fling you on my back like a sack of corn and carry you home, such was the resounding mirth."

"I remember the most of it—it weighs in the memory like sin in the guilty mind, as the bard would have it."

"Now which bard would that be?" asked Richmond, raising his eyebrows in a mischievous grin that made his already prominent chin protrude still further.

"Shakespeare of course. Is there another?"

"Why yes, the bard of Scotland—at least, that's what they're calling him. Have you not heard of Robert Burns, the ploughman poet? Not that he was ever a ploughman."

I confessed I had not, which seemed to set Richmond back some.

"He's a friend of mine from Ayrshire," he said. "He penned a book of verse, known as the Kilmarnock poems, that has been received with rapture by Edinburgh's literary lions. I've written to Rab to tell him to come to Edinburgh to let all the gay world see him, but he's having none of it and is set on a new life in Jamaica."

Richmond looked absolutely crestfallen. "It's really too bad," he continued. "There was never a man as blessed with brilliant repartee as Robert Burns. When we were younger, we used to meet as a secret bachelors' club, the Court of Equity, to report on and discuss the merits of the various scandals in the village. Burns was perpetual president and I, clerk of the court. The problem was that membership was restricted to those who were professed lovers of one or more of the female sex."

"And why would that be a problem?" I asked, still fuzzy-headed.

"Because the partridge that I brought to ground, the lovely Jenny Surgeoner, bore me a daughter nine months later, and I was forced on to the kirk's stool of repentance, clad in a black sackcloth gown. I headed to Edinburgh after the birth, still uncertain whether I'm running away or trying to make provision.

"Not that I was the first. Rab sat on the stool himself after his own bonnie wee hen got o'er-plump. But he was a rhymer even then and showed no sign of repentance. The court—Burns, myself and Jamie Smith as the prosecutor—held mock tribunals to discipline the hypocrites. Many of the poems in his Kilmarnock Edition are directed at the soapy sanctimony of folk like Willie Fisher, an elder in the kirk at Mauchline. I'll lend you my copy."

"I'd be delighted to read the musings of your ploughman friend," I said, thinking I'd rather be cursed with a chronic anxiety about the weather than waste my time on the bucolic scratchings of some unlettered peasant. What can I say? I was cocky and conceited, and I didn't know what I didn't know.

CHAPTER IV

I walked out of Baxter's Close to find the town already buzzing with people, as if all 80,000 of its inhabitants had decided to throng the High Street at one time.

The old walled city stretched from the castle at one end to Holyrood Palace at the other, a Royal Mile, with the low-lying Cowgate running parallel.

Big gurgling gutters filled with filth and refuse ran the length of the street; pigs poked their snouts around looking for a feast. Scavengers were clearing the pavements, filling wheelbarrows with domestic abominations that were tossed from high windows when St. Giles struck ten o'clock every evening. Richmond had warned me to be wary of the cry 'gardyloo,' which forewarned that the dirty luggies were about to be emptied onto the pavement below. Unwary or drunken pedestrians often wandered home dripping and ill-scented after being splashed by these flowers of Edinburgh.

The city was already astir; shopkeepers had opened. Their houses fronting the Royal Mile bore painted signs—a quarter loaf from the baker, a periwig at the barber's, a three-corner hat with the hatter. At right angles off the Mile ran wynds like upright streets from which spilled people of all grades and ranks. It seemed as if the sweep, the mechanic, the doctor, the noble and the judge all lived among one another, with the more affluent taking the upper storeys where the air was presumably fresher. A grubby-looking delivery boy emerged from one wynd, closely followed by a smart-looking lady wearing a silken plaid head scarf and a giant hooped dress, which she lifted above the filth through which she tripped nimbly in three-inch heels.

The street milled with porters carrying coals, fishwives selling their catch, men carrying water and barbers' boys dropping off new wigs. Sedan chairs swayed in all directions, carried by Highland porters who cursed loudly in Gaelic. Refined older ladies took the air, while advocates in gowns hustled to Parliament House to hear their latest cases. Remarkably, everyone seemed to know everyone else. Judges stopped to gossip with caddies, the messengers who knew all the goings on in Auld Reekie. As Richmond had said, "I've only been here a short while, but I have 50 friends within 500 yards."

I made my way to Carrubber's Close, just past the North Bridge, the construction of which 20 years prior had made it easier to access the New Town on the other side of the Nor Loch where the fashionable and the wealthy were starting to migrate. From the top of the bridge, you could make out the modern homes built of white stone. They were elegantly laid out in a uniform plan, a stark contrast to the irregularity and chaos of the Old Town.

Halfway down Carrubber's Close, I found a sign that read 'Society of Writers to His Majesty's Signet—Samuel Mitchelson, WS'. I knocked cautiously and wandered into a room where an ancient man with a grizzled wig, a yellow cloth coat and a deeply ruffled shirt was glowering over a column of figures, quill poised to pronounce the sum once the aged abacus had completed his calculation. He spared me not a second of his attention.

I removed my hat and stood there, wondering whether to say something or just turn tail and leave. Finally, a younger man with a trimmed periwig, a black coat and a scarlet waistcoat decorated with broad gold lace emerged from a room at the back of the office.

"Mr. Bruce, I presume? Come in, come in, we've been expecting you," he said rushing forward to pump my hand. "I'm David Balfour, apprentice to Mr. Mitchelson, who is attending the appeal of a case at the House of Lords in London and will be gone for some weeks. I have been empowered to act on all matters in his absence, so I will be instructing you for the next little while. Come in and make yourself comfortable."

He showed me to a desk in the corner and waved his hand toward the older gentleman. "This is old Mr. Beattie, who has been in this office since God was a boy. He was never a great one for repartee and has been increasingly less so as his hearing has declined," he said.

The senior gentleman appeared to be in the throes of transforming into some kind of Biblical hellion, his face contorted purple, as he wrestled with a mathematical challenge that appeared quite beyond him.

Balfour disappeared into the back again, and I sat wondering what to do next. The after-effects of the previous night resolved the dilemma as I was woken some time later by Balfour who bade me to follow him. As we walked out of the door, he asked me about my home and schooling. He already knew that the Laird of Galabank, an old friend of Mr. Mitchelson's, had recommended me as a pupil in law.

"Do you have any idea what a Writer of the Signet does?" he asked.

I confessed an uncertain insight that, in truth, was about as vague as my grasp of the mechanics of the female anatomy.

"Law agents are essentially middlemen," he said, "receiving money on behalf of clients and arranging that money be lent with interest to borrowers. You'll see how it all works when we meet the city councillor and the city clerk for our meridian."

"Meridian?"

"My dear boy, you are in the big world now. At one half hour past eleven, the gill-bells ring to tell the citizens of Edinburgh to head to the tavern to take their meridian—a gill of brandy, a tin of ale or, in the case of William Brodie, most likely a sherry.

"Hardly any sort of business is transacted but in a tavern. The etiquette is that he has the choice of beverage. One of the most important tasks of any pupil is to ensure that the tavern bill is passed on to the client, so please take note of all expenses incurred."

With that we swept into a low and dingy Bayle's Tavern and waited. At the next table, Balfour pointed out two magistrates splicing the rope—arranging the details of a hanging—over brandy.

"No function is too great to be celebrated in these insalubrious dark rooms," he said, "no functionary so lofty in rank that he will not mix in these unpretentious settings."

When the two city officials arrived, we were already well into our second sherry.

"Mr. Brodie and Mr. Hutton, two of Edinburgh's finest and most upstanding gentlemen. Our city is fortunate to have such men of calibre to govern its progress," said Balfour, who had become as servile as if the Lord President himself were among us.

The former was a short man with a dandyish look. He was dressed in a fine white suit with a blue silk waistcoat and gold-stitched embroidery, and his thick, black eyebrows were offset by brown, powdered hair. He was, apparently, a city councillor, deacon of a trades guild, a cabinetmaker and a pillar of the Edinburgh establishment.

He walked in with a swagger and talked in much the same manner.

His colleague, meanwhile, was a small, fussy-looking man who was every inch a clerk.

Balfour explained that an elderly female client wished to purchase annuities worth £1,000, at an interest rate of 10 per cent per annum, from the council. "She has a weak constitution, forever complaining about the cold, and last winter was much afflicted with rheumatism," he said with an unctuous shake of the head.

Balfour had already told me that Brodie would likely attempt to link his own business with that of the council—and so it proved.

"I'm distressed to hear of the poor health of your estimable client. One hopes she rallies when the weather turns more clement," he said. "The council is indeed sorely short of capital, and £1,000 would be of great utility. However, it troubles me that such an injurious rate of interest could be considered a risky investment for the council, given your client is a person of unknown character. But perhaps I could vouchsafe the request were I to meet with her, perhaps even transact with her. I am also a skilled cabinetmaker. Does she require any quality woodwork, perchance? I think that would be in order, don't you think, Mr. Hutton?" The latter mumbled his affirmation, clearly completely in the thrall of the beguiling Deacon Brodie.

We emerged into the cold 10 minutes later as Balfour rediscovered his poise, rubbing his hands in delight at having struck the deal.

"And that, my boy, is what a Writer of the Signet does," he said. "I had previously lodged the money with a banker at four per cent and have now more than doubled the return, all for the price of a new parlour cabinet.

"That greedy buzzard Brodie thinks our client has one foot in the grave, and hopes if she succumbs to her ailments and has no next of kin, the council might fall heir to her fortune by default. Little does he know she is as strong as Samson and will likely live until she's 90."

CHAPTER V

The following morning, a particularly blustery November day, Richmond and I wandered down the High Street together, on our way to our respective places of employment, when he stopped at the small post office in the Luckenbooths.

He emerged with a packet and read with rising anticipation. "It's from Burns," he said. "He's coming to Edinburgh to throw off a second impression of his book." He looked as happy as a dog with a stick.

It was three nights later that I wandered into Johnnie Dowie's and encountered Burns and, later, met the Crochallan Fencibles in the flesh at Dawnie Douglas' tavern. As the mirth was loud—the stories and jests broad— the price paid the following morning was prodigious.

I woke early and headed downstairs, keen to intercept the intriguing new arrival in our midst. Burns had arranged to stay with Richmond so he could settle his affairs in the capital. He was only seven years older than me, yet his life seemed to exist in an altogether more exulted and rarified sphere. Richmond had told me that not only did Burns have one bastard child who was now being raised by the poet's mother, he had twins from another local lass. Burns himself had told us that on his ride to Edinburgh from Ayrshire, he'd stopped overnight at a farm near Lanark where all the farmers in the district came to shake his hand.

"You may henceforth see my birthday inserted among the wonderful events," he had joked. "By all probability I shall soon be the tenth most worthy and eighth most wise man in the world."

The fame of Caledonia's bard was blossoming, and here I was living in the same crumbling boarding house. Poetry had always been remote and ancient—Homeric epics and Chaucerian tales—but here was a poet revered for writing chiefly in the Scots dialect about a world I knew. I was star-struck—and I hadn't yet read a word.

Mrs. Carfrae buzzed around the kitchen, lamenting the decline of standards, particularly among young gentlemen. "It's a degenerate age of vice and folly," she fussed. "I've told Mr. Richmond the godless poet can stay under this roof only until he can arrange his own accommodation. He mocks the kirk and the old ways, or that's what I hear anyways."

"Have you read any of his verse, Mrs. Carfrae?"

"I would never. My reading is reserved for the Holy Book. But Mrs. Brown, the fishwife, has a cousin in Ayrshire who said this Robert Burns had to pay a guinea fine and sit on the stool of repentance for his fornication. On the day of vengeance, the Lord will smite him down. And you, too, if you are taken in by his devilish powers."

With that, she swept out of the kitchen, put on her hat and coat and left the house, off to give some other poor soul the benefit of her simmering bigotry. As soon as she had gone, there was a commotion on the stairs as Burns and Richmond tumbled through the kitchen, pulling me in their wake.

We staggered against a brisk east wind, across the High Street and into a coffee house on the northeast corner of Parliament Square, famous, Richmond said, for the opposition of its patrons to the union of the parliaments.

Burns said he had arranged to meet with Peter Hill, one of the Fencibiles from the previous evening who, besides being a prodigious drinker, was first clerk to William Creech, the town's most prominent publisher.

"When I said I had no introductions in this town, I was being less than frank," said Burns. "The master of my lodge in Ayrshire has written ahead to a fellow countryman here, and he has secured me an audience with the Earl of Glencairn. And, by pure chance, I now have a connection to a man who may be able to publish a new edition of my poetry. I've no great temptation to be intoxicated with the cup of prosperity, but being great would be charming," he laughed and then stared at me. Despite the obvious toll taken by the previous night's claret, his eyes glowed when he spoke with feeling or interest. He was indeed a dazzling presence, as even Mrs. Carfrae had divined.

Hill, a slight, pale man in his early 30s, arrived and flopped down in a chair.

"Mr. Hill, you look like you have not yet digested the vine from our evening on manoeuvres with the Crochallan corps," said Richmond.

"I am indeed a monument for the vengeance laid in store for the wicked. But it was a chance encounter, Mr.

Burns. I have mentioned to my esteemed, if penurious, employer, Mr. Creech, that you are in Edinburgh with the intent of publishing an enlarged edition of your work. I hesitate to say he salivated, but it's enough to suggest he is extremely eager to make your acquaintance," said Hill.

He explained that Creech owned the bookshop and library in the Luckenbooths on the High Street, where eminent citizens gathered to see the newest books from London and the freshest arrivals from the country. Burns was already the talk of the town, he said.

He invited us to join him on the short trip to Creech's shop. We walked into an ill-lit lobby that opened on to a room with an elaborately stuccoed ceiling, a finely carved and massive marble mantelpiece, and oak-panelled walls. The place reeked of ink, and deep in the bowels of the building, there was the clatter of a press. But in this grand room three men sat around taking snuff and chatting amiably. It sounded like word of Burns' arrival was indeed the news of the day.

"He has native dignity and is the very fissure of his profession—strong and coarse but with a most enthusiastic heart of love as well," said an older, dignified-looking gentleman.

An extremely well-dressed man in his early middle age exclaimed, "He seems a boon companion, though he can startle with a dash of libertinism, which will keep some readers distant."

"I agree," said a younger but no less distinguished-looking man. "Yet the poems are simple, manly and independent. They are strongly expressive of conscious genius and worth, without indicating forwardness, arrogance or vanity. Having hosted the poet to dinner at my country seat in AyrshirÆy, I can testify they are the mirror image of the man who wrote them."

Burns obviously felt it would be impertinent to listen to such laudatory comments without making his presence known and stepped forward. "Very kind of you to say so, Dr. Stewart. It's a pleasure to see your countenance again and to hear your continued patronage," said the poet.

Once all the introductions were concluded, it emerged that Burns was being feted by not just the pillars of the Scottish establishment but the buttresses, too. The older man was the Reverend Dr. Hugh Blair, chair of rhetoric at Edinburgh University and a key figure in the attempt to un-Scotchify the nation. The well-dressed middle-aged man was Henry Mackenzie, author of the great novel *The Man of Feeling* and editor of *The Lounger* newspaper, while the younger man was Dr. Dugald Stewart, chair of moral philosophy at the university.

Soon a short, fastidious man in black silk breeches and powdered hair entered the room—William Creech—and Burns had found his publisher. Creech was a strange creature who always checked his timepiece as if he had to rush off to a much more important assignation. But for now, the poet had his full attention. Creech recommended a new subscription and promised to subscribe to 500 copies himself.

Blair, who seemed to regard himself as the judge and jury of literary merit, suggested to Burns that he should write in the King's English to broaden his audience. He further made the imperious suggestion that the poet might want to look further afield for subject matter—Biblical or classical themes, for example.

Burns' response exhibited confidence but not presumption. He was polite but insistent that he relied on direct observation to give his verse a measure of authenticity. His poetry was as natural as a trout in the river, he said, and if the Maker had seen fit to give him a voice, he was obliged to use it. Blair harrumphed but retreated in the knowledge he'd been beaten at his own game.

It was apparent that Burns was keen to measure his native ability against these eminent professors, and he put his points more forcibly than was perhaps conventional. When Creech ventured that Thomas Gray's elegy was overwrought, Burns leapt to his fellow poet's defence. "Sir, I now perceive that a man may be an excellent judge of poetry by square and rule and, after all, be a damned blockhead," he said.

If Creech took exception, he didn't show it. But then he had just signed up the most talked about man in Scotland.

Later, in Johnnie Dowie's, I asked the poet why he felt the need to prove himself. "It's a weakness, perhaps a jealousy of anyone richer or of more consequence than me," he sighed into his claret. "But fortune has made them powerful and me impotent, has given them patronage and me dependence. It gnaws at me."

The wine had emboldened me. "Yet you are prepared to prostrate yourself before them, a court jester for the lords and their ladies," I said.

He lifted his eyes and pierced me. "Young Bruce," he said, "every guinea I have currently has a five-guinea errand. I have tender concerns, ties and claims upon me that unnerve my courage and wither my powers of disdain. You are dazzled by the regard in which these great men appear to hold me. But it is novelty, and while novelty may attract the attention of mankind for a while, the time is not too distant when the tide of popularity will retreat and leave me a barren waste of sand on which to descend at my leisure to my former station."

I protested, "But you haven't even struck off your second edition yet. Your greatest triumphs are ahead of you."

"Perhaps. But I do not say this with affected modesty. I see the consequence is unavoidable and I am prepared for it," he said.

CHAPTER VI

I'd have walked into Hell with Burns just to hear him describe the journey.

He lent me a copy of his Kilmarnock Edition, and I devoured it. Growing up I had no older siblings, just two annoying younger brothers who were forever bestowing their unwelcome attentions upon me. I think I came to behave in a similar fashion around the poet, although he was always courteous to me. I found myself tying my hair back the same way he did. I bought myself a pair of knee-high leather boots that looked like his and began to wear lace at the neck and cuff as he did.

I badgered him to read to me his tale of the lives of differing social classes, The Twa Dogs. I pestered him to tell me about the bawdy adventures he, Jamie Smith and Jock Richmond enjoyed in Ayrshire as 'the rattling squad'. I tormented him until he told me the inspiration for his tale of Halloween. He had a retentive memory, he said, and could still recall the stories of ghosts, fairies, witches and warlocks he'd been told as a boy by an elderly relative. "To this hour, in my nocturnal rambles, I sometimes keep a sharp lookout in suspicious places," he said.

Lying on my cramped chaff bed, the poems added a palette of bright paint to the monochrome world I'd known in Galabank. Some of the themes were familiar, but in Burns' world there was more life, more colour, more fun. I'd grown up something of a recluse, worked like a galley slave by my father who was set on me making something of myself in the world. He had hired a tutor to teach me arithmetic, astronomy, natural history and geography. I was a good student but my father was irascible and unrelenting, while my mother was distant and preoccupied with my two younger brothers. I spent so much time on my own, I lacked much native wit around others. The future was a bottomless pit, and I often felt I was not equipped for the struggles of life.

In my early manhood I thought I'd found my course. I would ride to harvest festivals and dances in Annan and got my first flesh wounds from Cupid's arrows. Lorna Campbell was her name, and her voice made my pulse thrum a furious percussion. I never got much closer than picking nettle stings from her hand, but she at least aided me with the stammering awkwardness I had around the fairer sex.

I possessed certain gifts. I was manly enough. I had bookish knowledge and abilities of observation and remark, when pressed. It turned out that my father had equipped me with the weapons to fight the progressive struggle of life. But any intoxicated vanity deserted me when I arrived in Edinburgh, and the poet's presence overwhelmed any sense of self I had developed. I admired him and strove to emulate him.

Burns spent much of his time that December touring the homes of the gentry as he tried to sell subscriptions to his newly printed Edinburgh Edition. This endeavour was aided greatly by a glowing review of the earlier

Kilmarnock Edition in the pages of *The Lounger*, where Henry Mackenzie referred to "surprising effects of original genius." If the poet wasn't engaged in conversation at Creech's bookshop, he was before the Canongate Lodge of Freemasons with the Earl of Glencairn. It became a patriotic act to subscribe to Burns' second edition.

On one occasion I accompanied him to the house of the eminent philosopher Professor Adam Ferguson, where Burns was much affected by a painting of a soldier lying dead in the snow, his dog sitting in misery on one side and his widow and child on the other. The poet actually shed a tear and asked whose verses were engraved underneath the painting. No one knew until a slight, lame lad of about 15 or so whispered in my ear that the words came from a half-forgotten poem called The Justice of the Peace by Langhorne. I mentioned it to Burns, who took the boy aside and thanked him. "You'll be a man yet, sir," he said, patting him on the back. The boy has indeed grown to be a man and one of quite substance—his name is Walter Scott, whose Waverley novels have caused such a stir of late.

Burns' presence was most coveted at parties and suppers that winter season. He had tea with the boisterous Duchess of Gordon, long remembered for having ridden down the Royal Mile on the back of a sow.

He was also a regular guest in Lord Monboddo's abode, where claret was served from flasks garlanded with roses. Burns told me he was charmed with Monboddo's daughter Eliza. "There's been nothing like her since Milton's Eve on the first day of her existence," he said. He even included a stanza in tribute to her beauty in his Address to Edinburgh that so thrilled the blustering burgesses of the capital, even if its literary merits were questionable.

But this is where the bard's strange sorcery failed him for once—his rustic spell held no sway over women of a higher social station, who were tickled and not a little tantalized by the manly ploughman poet. But he had a very inadequate idea of how to connect with refined ladies, and they even fewer sensibilities when it came to dealing with a force of nature like him, beyond keeping his charms at arm's length.

His failure to reconcile himself to this gulf of rank and manners led to Clarinda, heartbreak and the rift that divided us.

The problem was that Burns, by his own admission, was afflicted with a tinder heart eternally lit by some goddess or another. But his advances to the likes of Eliza Monboddo had scant prospect of breaching the bulwark erected by respectable society to keep those of us of less noble birth at bay.

Thus, in between his brief forays into polite society, he spent most evenings with the Crochallan Fencibles in Dawnie Douglas' tavern. Charles Hay, one of the town's foremost advocates, was not the only member who elevated hilarity and friendship above all else. "Drinking is my occupation, law my amusement," he said. For Burns, Willie Dunbar's epic consumption was worthy of a special form of grace, and he was forever after known as Rattlin' Roarin' Willie.

When held against some of our contemporaries, we were the very model of decorum and fine manners. The gentlemen of the Boar Club, for example, spent their time acting like pigs; Facer Club members had to throw their drinks in their own faces if they were unable to drain their measure.

The libertines at The Beggar's Benison not only

drank and sang, it was said they satisfied their amorous propensities with naked women.

By comparison, bawdy songs and good company were tame fare and provided ballast to the turbulent seas on which we all sailed. Yet none of this helped slake Burns' thirst for the fairer sex, nor mine for that matter.

We had arrived in a time and place removed from Burns' experience being a Sunday laughing stock in Ayrshire. The fear of bastard children and love poxes remained strong, but dread of hellfire and public humiliation was gone. Mrs. Carfrae was an exception to the wave of religious tolerance that had swept the capital. People began to define morality in a more personal way, living according to Samuel Johnson's maxim 'That every man should regulate his actions by his own conscience'.

It was considered natural that men would pursue sexual opportunity. Unfortunately, women, particularly women of station, were considered instinctively more virtuous—and behaved as such.

"My rhetoric seems to have lost its effect on the lively half of mankind," lamented Burns one night in Johnnie Dowie's. "Love and poetry have become strangers of late."

It began to perturb him that high society had grown to consider him a form of salon entertainment. He turned down one hostess by saying he'd be delighted to accept her invitation but only if she also asked the Learned Pig, then performing card tricks as part of a travelling novelty show in the Grassmarket.

The only solution for the devoted slaves of delicious passion, like Burns had become and I hoped to become, was to seek companions who were more flexible in their personal morality.

CHAPTER VII

The task was not Herculean—there were whores and jades all over town. *Ranger's Impartial List of the Ladies of Pleasure of Edinburgh* even provided a guide to several dozen of the capital's most hospitable courtesans.

Several times I had seen a shapely ankle disappearing up the stairwell that led to the apartments above my room. One evening in late January, I contrived an introduction to the noisy neighbours by waiting in the close outside Mrs. Carfrae's entrance until I heard a door upstairs being slammed. I made a great fuss of locking my own door and timed my exit perfectly to encounter a small, genteel-looking lass of about 20 years of age with blonde hair and a slight squint in her right eye. She was dressed in a brown riding outfit, tight around a lithe-looking torso, then hooped at the waist, all topped off by a jaunty green bonnet. Such outfits were not cheap. I stepped back to let her pass, doffing my felt hat as I bent deeply.

"Evening, madam. John Bruce, at your service."

She stopped and regarded me with a pinched smile. "Pleased to make your acquaintance, Mr. Bruce. I'm Peggy, Peggy Alexander. Now would it be you that bangs on the ceiling every night with a broom when my friends and I are practicing our oratorio?"

"Ah, that would be my landlady, Mrs. Carfrae—she's a light sleeper. Oratorio?" I asked, confused.

"Of course. Whatever did you think all that chanting and howling was? Oh yes, my friends and I are preparing for a recital of the *Messiah*. I just love *The Passion* in Part Two, don't you?" she said with more than a hint of salaciousness. At this point she skipped off laughing, leaving me tongue-tied and twisted.

I wandered down to Johnnie Dowie's where Richmond, Nicol and William Smellie had taken up residence. It had emerged, by pure serendipity, that Smellie owned a printing shop at the head of Anchor Close, where he had previously printed works by authors as esteemed as Adam Smith, and he had now agreed to cast off Burns' second edition.

The poet himself entered in damp spirits just after I arrived. He ordered a bumper of brandy for each of us.

"I would prefer a small glass," I offered, trying to at least dilute the spirits flowing through my veins and crushing my brain every morning.

"But what's the point, sir?" remonstrated Burns. "You will drink two glasses to my one bumper. You remind me of a lass in Kyle who said she would rather be kissed twice bare-headed than once with her bonnet on."

While we waited for our drinks, I mentioned to Burns my encounter with Peggy Alexander.

"Ah, one of the gay girls. I've met another of them," he said.

"Are they whores?" I asked.

"More like concubines. Yes, in that they are paid for intimacy. No, in that they are not abandoned pieces. They have generous patrons, which puts them out of your range for now."

He said one of the so-called gay girls was black and had escaped slavery on a boat from the Caribbean that had arrived at the Port of Leith. "Miss Ruthven is comely, with good teeth and an agreeable nature," he said. "I'm told she loves the sport very well. But she is mistress to a lord."

As he led me to The Coffin, in the back of the tavern, to join the others, he placed his hand on my shoulder.

"I am, you know, a veteran in these campaigns, so let me give you some advice," said Burns. "Steer clear of the jades because where's the sport in that? Find a plump, young serving wench, and try for intimacy as soon as you feel the first symptoms of passion. This makes the most of the little entertainment likely in such a coupling."

He handed me a slim volume—*The Complaint: or, Night-Thoughts on Life, Death, and Immortality* by Edward Young. "Read this," he said. "'Procrastination is the thief of time; year after year it steals till all are fled.' That applies to houghmagandie as much as any other field of endeavour."

When we arrived in The Coffin, Smellie and Nicol were engaged in heated argument, while Richmond appeared to being doing his best to distance himself from the debate. It surfaced that Smellie had edited the first-ever Encyclopedia Britannica, which had appeared in 100 or so instalments some 20 years prior, and which Nicol was now claiming was littered with inaccuracies and wild speculations.

"There is a generation of young minds that have been addled by some of the nonsense you penned in that weighty tome," said the schoolmaster with his customary diplomacy.

"Well at least I have desisted. You are still ruining our youth," replied the dishevelled printer.

"Let's take what you said about tobacco. There's not a gentleman here that doesn't enjoy his snuff—and all the lower orders smoke like chimneys. Yet you said it leads to neuro....what?"

"Neurodegeneration. It dries up the brain to a little black lump containing mere membranes," said Smellie.

"But where's your proof, man? If there were anything wrong with it, we'd all be dead. No wonder the university overlooked you for Professor of Natural History. I've never heard anything so ridiculous. Tobacco's as harmless as a garter snake."

Burns chimed in. "The entry with which I take issue is his four-word description of women: 'The female of man'. I would suggest Willie gravelly underestimated their fascinating witchcraft.

"On the subject of which I have penned some lines to an old Scottish jig that I would like to introduce to the next gathering of the Crochallan Fencibles. I have christened it My Wife's a Wanton Wee Thing, and it celebrates all those married ladies who enjoy a light horse gallop in the air."

Everyone around the table, even Nicol, grabbed mouthfuls of laughter and all the ills of life ebbed away.

"Rab, you should collect all these scattered verses and publish them," suggested Richmond.

The poet rubbed his chin, deep in thought. "Maybe I should at that, maybe I should," he said.

CHAPTER VIII

Having adopted me, Burns was intent on rounding out my education. He knocked on my door one evening and asked me if I was free to join him.

I grabbed my hat and coat and followed him as he strode determinedly down the High Street.

"Where are we going?" I wondered.

"Merryland."

"The Americas?"

"No—M-e-r-r-y-land. It has hills like Lebanon, valleys like Eden and a garden of delight," he laughed.

He veered left up Stamp Office Close to Fortune's Tavern, whereupon we were ushered into a private back room. A resplendent black woman in a plain, silk dishabille greeted the poet.

"Mr. Burns, I'm glad you could make it," she said. "And this must be Mr. Bruce. Welcome to the Wig Club. Come in and meet my patron, the Lord Protector of the Wig, Lord Moray." She spoke with a mellifluous accent, the like of which I had never heard, all the while exposing ivory white teeth and an expanse of bare ebony skin, the like of which I had never seen.

She mock-curtsied before an ample middle-aged gentleman who looked as if he was so pleased with himself he might drink his own bathwater. He glanced down his nose at Burns and me before turning to the company on his left.

The room was cramped with perhaps another half dozen men and two women, one of whom was my petite neighbour, Miss Alexander. The men appeared to be prosperous gentlemen of commerce and law; I noted the attendance of Deacon Brodie. The ladies were dressed in similar fashion to the beautiful black woman, who I took to be Miss Ruthven.

As the men chatted, the women served two-penny ale and penny pies. Brodie came over to where Burns and I were standing, shook my hand and introduced himself to the poet. "How do things stand with you, Mr. Burns? I hear we are neighbours. My house on Brodie Close sits across from your lodgings. Word travels fast in this small town," he said knowingly. "I hope you enjoy the evening. I prefer the dice or fighting gamecocks, but I confess I can't resist the lure of a pretty wench, especially one the colour of Black Cork ale." He laughed heartily before moving to the next group.

When he was out of earshot, Burns whispered to me, "He may have the appearance of a gentleman, but that one is not all he seems. I am not often wrong about people, and he is like a woman with too much paint on her face, as if he is hiding something. Mark me on that."

By then the Lord Protector was ready to commence proceedings. He begged everyone's attention, and Miss Ruthven handed him a wooden box from which he removed a tatty old hairpiece. His was an undistinguished voice that struggled for passion, as if he were saying grace at a kirk supper.

"Gentlemen, welcome to the Wig Club. This artifact was donated by Charles the second—the merry king himself—as a token of his esteem for the riotous times he enjoyed in Scotia. It is made entirely from the pubic hair of his mistresses, save for those hairs that have been offered by new members from their own mistresses." Lord Moray said all this with a straight face, while I gazed at the grizzled mane with a mix of incredulity and consternation. Burns, meanwhile, seemed to have been seized by an acute anxiety about his boots and could not be persuaded to look at the speaker or any other members of the assembled throng while he emitted stifled yelps.

Lord Moray continued, "We are on the threshold of a new age, gentlemen, one free of religious dogma. Sex, in my opinion, is as worthy of scientific inquiry as other areas of natural history. So I propose to examine the subject of masturbation and its supposed links to insanity before our posture girls here guide us through the female physiology."

He blathered and skited in this vein for several more minutes before the three ladies emerged to stand at the front of the room completely naked save a face mask they held in one hand. The sense was they were to be looked at rather than touched, but since I could not even stand up, this troubled me not. All three were beautiful, the last one young, slim and red of hair, both at collar and cuff.

There was much murmured discussion and pointing by the members while they wandered around the three ladies as if at a horse fair. In due course Lord Moray spoke again. "We will now initiate the two new members," he said. "Gentlemen, if you will come forward and kiss the wig."

"Begging your pardon, Lord Protector?" said Burns, scarcely able to contain himself.

"You must kiss the wig and contribute a hair from the nether regions of your own mistress to embellish the thatch," said Lord Moray as if it were the most obvious thing in the world. "Since I believe your young friend remains a novice in these affairs, perhaps our posture girls could assist."

I blushed the colour of claret as I walked to the front of the room. Burns was before me, almost nonchalant, making his way to the third girl. "Would you do me the honour, Miss…," he laughed.

"Why, charmed, Mr. Burns. Your fame precedes you," she trilled as she plucked a curly red tress from below her midriff and handed it to him. "And it's Miss Cameron. Meg Cameron."

He walked up to Lord Moray, who was wearing the wretched nest, kissed it lightly and slipped the hair into the thatch. He then turned to the members and bowed deeply.

"Gentlemen and especially ladies," he said, "I thank you for inviting me to your club. Forgive me for saying, there is altogether an over-abundance of thinking and an absence of feeling in the contemplation of Aphrodite and her arts. So I beg your pardon and bid you adieu." He walked out amid rumblings of discontent.

I followed as the now boisterous gathering egged me on. I walked through their midst toward Peggy Alexander, who was extending a pinched thumb and forefinger toward me. I gathered the hair, pecked the wig and strode out into the tavern to the sound of much hilarity at my back.

"May neither your prick nor purse e'er fail you," I heard Deacon Brodie cry from within as I emerged on the close to find Burns heaving with laughter.

"Lord Moray is a man to whom fate gave a full purse and nature gave an empty head," he chuckled some more, putting an arm around me. "Little does our godly matron, Mrs. Carfrae, suspect that the wenching blades and filthy jades overhead perform their sport wearing a periwig made from the bush of the Merry Monarch's doxy."

I nodded but could scarcely speak. I could hardly reveal that my knowledge of the female geography, including the very existence of hair, had been as dubious as those who insist the earth is flat.

CHAPTER IX

It was some days later that I saw the poet again. He had been busy not only making arrangements for his second edition but running hither and thither collecting fragments of bawdy songs that he intended to collate into some kind of package. In this mission and another that were to become his life's work, Burns was accompanied by James Johnson, a thin, bookish engraver who had a shop on Lady Stair Close, near our apartments, and was a fellow Crochallan Fencible. Johnson had the notion of collecting the words and music of all the old Scots ballads and already had an edition of his Scots Musical Museum on the presses. He asked Burns to become involved, so as Burns scoured for bawd, he also searched for old airs and verses that he could patch together, often with a few lines he had lying around, as if waiting for just such a purpose.

I had agreed to join the poet and another Fencible, the local surgeon Sandy Wood, for a stroll up through King's Park to Arthur's Seat, where on a clear day there was a panorama of 12 of the principal Scottish counties. This was just such a bright, crisp, early spring day.

We congregated outside Wood's house at the Royal Exchange square. The surgeon was a strange, rangy coof. He used to have a pet sheep that followed him around on his house calls, and he was well-named Lang Sandy—he and everyone in his family was over six feet tall. When he emerged to meet us, he pointed to the steps leading to the Wood household. "Take care, gentlemen. You are standing on our very own Giant's Causeway," he said with a rumbling laugh.

Revelling in the sun and light, we wandered down the Royal Mile, exiting the city before the now empty Holyrood Palace, and strode up the grassy slopes. "We are a poor excuse for a country, one that has so tamely handed over prince and parliament," mused Burns.

Sandy asked the poet about his plans for the future. For all his native wit, Burns was as constant as a weather vane—one day leaving for Jamaica, the next setting forth for Edinburgh; one day buying a farm in Dumfries, the next becoming a tax collector. His tendency to go with the prevailing wind was apparent in his private life, too. He told the surgeon about the guinea fine and buttock hire he'd had to pay for the lass, Bess, who was now being raised by his mother.

"I had commenced as a fornicator with that bonny hen Lizzie Paton, and it cost me a time on the stool of repentance. But even wearing that black sackcloth gown, I had no remorse," he said.

Then there was the other girl, Jean Armour, who had repaid his amorous advances double with twins, though only the boy had survived. He had been forced to dodge home to home to avoid the warrant with which Armour's enraged father intended as a means to throw the poet in jail.

"Her mother was worse. May Hell string the arm of death to throw the fatal dart, and all the winds of warring elements rouse the infernal flame to welcome her approach," he said with malice. "I engaged in all kinds of dissipation and riot trying to forget that girl. In truth, I was on the verge of breakdown."

Of all his liaisons, it was clear even from this exchange that Jean held a special place in his heart. "She has the handsomest figure, the sweetest temper, the soundest constitution and the kindest heart in the country," he said. "I doubt, with the exception of the Scripture, she has spent more than five minutes with prose or verse. But she is loyal and has pardoned my many offences."

He said he had courted her two years prior when she fell pregnant. He had given her a paper that constituted a marriage contract, but her father annulled the union, a fact that was confirmed by Mauchline Kirk Session and which established he was a bachelor.

"'Twas as well. I have a sore warfare in this world. The Devil, the world and the flesh are three formidable foes. The first, I generally try to fly from; the second, alas, generally flies from me; but the third is my plague—worse than the 10 plagues of Egypt," he said to Sandy as I tagged along behind them.

Amid all this folly, Burns had struck a rich vein of poetic inspiration, and the poet was clear that it was his intention to repair much of the damage he'd done with the proceeds. He said he'd left the profit from *The Kilmarnock Edition* with his brother who was looking after their mother, the baby Bess and four siblings in Ayrshire. He stopped and looked at Wood.

"I've never been a rogue, but I've been a fool my whole life, the victim of too much imprudence and many follies," he said.

He was prone to fine words, likely meant when he said them, but his warm enthusiasm was currently being reserved for Meg Cameron, the posture girl, who it later emerged was one of Creech's servants. She merely posed naked for strange men in her spare hours.

Somehow, Burns had sneaked her past Mrs. Carfrae and imposed on Richmond and me to share a bed so he'd be left free in the other room. It made me even more acutely aware of my own lack of amorous assignations.

When we reached the summit, we lay and marvelled at the view: to our right, Auld Reekie, the Forth and beyond that Fife; to our left, the softly rolling hills of Lothian.

Burns, as always, had to fill the silence. "I've been reflecting on a new pursuit for the Fencibles—we draw lots and then write an epitaph for whichever esteemed comrade we pick. The condition on the adoption of my trivial pursuit is that I get Willie Nicol, since I have already penned his eulogy:

'Ye maggots, feed on Nicol's brain,
For few sic feasts you've gotten;
And fix your claws in Nicol's heart,
For deil a bit o't's rotten.'"

That set us off backslapping and laughing all the way down the hill that looks like a mountain. I found myself walking alongside Burns as we entered the city. I confided in him that I thought I was in love.

"Congratulations, lad. Love is the alpha and omega of human enjoyment. Have you taken my advice on pushing for intimacy at the onset of passion?"

I confessed I'd met the girl in question but twice and had no real opportunity at intimacy—or not what anyone of sound mind would recognize as such a thing.

"Well what kind of pursuit is that? Who is this bonny wee bird?"

"Peggy Alexander," I said sheepishly.

"Peggy...you don't mean...? This is a town filled with goddesses, and you have to fall in love with a fallen angel."

"You said she wasn't a bawd, that she was a gay girl, a concubine."

"Discard what I said. She's a strumpet. Reconcile yourself to this— She's currently enjoying the pintle of milord Moray. It may not be as plump and firm as yours, but unlike yours, it has a gold pot to piss in."

It was all true, but it ruined all the benefits of our constitutional. I returned to my room, quite deflated.

CHAPTER X

In truth, I had little reason to complain about a world that had, in general, been kind to me—I enjoyed my just desserts. But on evenings like this one, I felt pangs of disappointment and nostalgia for my formative life at Galabank, or perhaps, a false nostalgia for a past that never really happened, one where my father had been warmer and my mother more loving. I craved compassion and generosity, yet it seemed in short supply. Even Burns, who had called me an invaluable treasure because he could talk nonsense to me without forfeiting his esteem, had derided me.

It's not as though I wasn't aware that Peggy was unobtainable to a poor apprentice at law. Nor was it as if I had made a conscious decision to fall hopelessly in love with my lordship's tumble. She was forever with me, not least because I could hear her dancing the featherbed jig every night through the thin ceiling.

I was reflecting on this very matter when I felt a light sprinkle of plaster fall on my head, followed by yet more and a light hammering noise. I watched as a crack spread across the ceiling and a knifepoint appeared, rotating to make a small hole that was first filled by a large brown eye then by full lips.

"Brother Bruce," whispered a voice that was unmistakably that of the poet. "If you recall I advised you on the alpha and omega of human enjoyment. I regret I was overly harsh with you earlier, so if you'd care to repair to your neighbours' rooms overhead, I've arranged a peacemaker."

I didn't need to be asked twice. I ran out of Mrs. Carfrae's door and sprinted the two flights up. Peggy answered the door. Her blonde hair was piled high, falling in ringlets on her right shoulder. She wore gold earrings and a gold necklace over a low-cut, lacy pink concoction that framed her pale skin beautifully. Even her slight squint was adorable.

"Mr. Bruce, I hardly recognized you with my clothes on," she said.

I turned pink and fumbled to take her hand to purse my lips to it. Over her shoulder I saw Burns and Meg Cameron disappearing into an adjacent room. Peggy ushered me into a low-ceilinged, ill-lit parlour.

"Milord Moray has left town for a few days," she said. "He appears to have appreciated that he is depriving one of his villages of an idiot and has retired to his ancestral lands to fill the vacancy. I will endeavour to struggle on without him. Meanwhile, Mr. Burns has told of your small affection for me and has suggested he may remember me in verse if I am kind to you."

"He is a true friend," I mumbled. "And you as well, uh, Miss Alexander..."

"Peggy, please."

"And you...Peggy. What brings you to your present...circumstance?"

"My circumstance as a woman of pleasure, you mean?"

I half-nodded, half-choked.

"Well, my father was a prosperous merchant until he drank and gambled the family's money away and then did the decent thing by dying. I was a masterless woman, trading silks and cloth until I was robbed and left destitute. That was when I met the Lord Moray, who had been an associate of my father. He is aware that I am using him quite as fully as he is using me."

"He's quite...well...older."

"He is old and he is dull. If he were drowning, someone else's life would pass before his eyes. The only interesting thing about him is that ratty old wig. But then a full purse is never short of friends."

"Peggy, I hope Burns does write a verse for you. There are none in Edinburgh as fair as you, at least in my experience, which is to be sure far from extensive."

"So I may not be that fair after all?" she teased.

"Now you're twisting my words. And words matter. In the end, nothing endures but words, and if you appear in one of Burns' works, you'll live forever."

She smiled sweetly, rose slowly, took my hand and led me gently toward her boudoir.

CHAPTER XI

Richmond and I were ranged around a bowl in Johnnie Dowie's tavern some nights on, quite content with life, when Burns entered in a rage.

He had just come from dinner at the Reverend Dr. Blair's house, and we concluded swiftly that events had not gone well.

Burns arranged himself with a bumper of claret. "Vain pomp and glory of this world, I hate you. What merits have these wretches had, or what demerit have I had, that they enter this world with the sceptre of rule and key of riches, while I am forced to be the victim of their pride?"

"Rab, those are your patrons and sponsors you speak of. What's ailing you?" asked Richmond.

The poet explained that not only was the gulf in rank foiling his advances on the capital's most eligible maids, his rustic manners had inadvertently insulted his host. The Reverend Blair had asked in which public place Burns had received greatest gratification. The poet replied in the High Church of St. Giles, which was greeted with murmurs of approval around the table since Blair was the minister there. But those good notices were quickly replaced by an uncomfortable silence when he added his preference as preacher was his friend Dr. William Greenfield, an associate in the pulpit at St. Giles.

"The conversation was laboured thereafter," said Burns. "But the world owes poets a larger latitude in the laws of propriety than the sober sons of judgment and prudence."

He said Blair was trying to persuade him not to include a certain work in his Edinburgh Edition, one that Burns himself had already considered to "free" to include in his Kilmarnock version.

"You remember *The Jolly Beggars*, Jock? It was the cantata I penned after we witnessed the jollity among the company of beggars one night in Poosie Nansie's tavern in Mauchline."

"I do," replied Richmond. "We were much taken at the ongoings of the old maimed redcoat who got up and belted out the Soldier's Joy."

He turned to me to explain. "There was a raggle-taggle band of beggars in front of the fire in Agnes Gibson's dosshouse. One old soldier, missing an arm and a leg, sang to his love, and she replied with a song of her own. Rab interjected himself into the proceedings with a verse, and later he wrote a dramatic tribute to a life of pleasure."

He turned back to Burns. "It's scarcely a wonder that Dr. Blair is not pressing for its inclusion. He may be a man or reason, but he's hardly a man of romance. That work was a celebration of joyous sex," said Richmond.

"More a defence of the right of people to live as they might wish," said Burns.

I asked him to give me a flavour of the verse and he obliged:

"A fig for those by law protected!
Liberty's a glorious feast!
Courts for cowards were erected,
Churches built to please the priest."

"I can see why a minister of the kirk might consider that dangerous entertainment, even in days when the old bigotry is losing its hold," I said.

The fight seemed to go out of Burns at that. "When Dr. Blair interests himself in my welfare, or still more, when he descends from his pinnacle and greets me as on equal ground, my heart overflows with liking. But when he neglects me, I say to myself with scarcely an emotion, 'What care I for him or his pomp?'"

But it was clear that he did care and was deeply wounded by his failure to surmount the glass wall between himself and polite society. As Burns settled into his cups, his mood grew darker.

"It is a cruel satire that we are discussing a paen to pleasure," he said. "The truth is human existence in its most favourable situation does not abound with pleasure. Despite the evidence you have seen hitherto, John, I am plagued by blue devils. Richmond knows.

"I feel a secret wretchedness—wandering stabs of remorse, which never fail to settle in my vitals like vultures. Even in my hour of social mirth, my gaiety is the madness of an intoxicated criminal under the hands of the executioner."

To a man like Burns it was clear that Edinburgh was a foreign land. The town was at the forefront of a movement: 'I think therefore I am.' But Burns was governed by an altogether different constitution: 'I feel therefore I am.'

He said he was considering an offer from Patrick Miller, a director of the Bank of Scotland and one of his earliest benefactors, to take a lease on a farm on his estate near Dumfries.

"He's no judge of land, and though I'm sure he means to favour me, he may hand me an advantageous bargain that ruins me. But once I have finished correcting proofs on my Edinburgh Edition at Smellie's establishment, I think I will take a ride south to inspect the property."

By this time, he was very drunk and inconsolable. "I have a hundred times wished one could resign life as an officer resigns a commission. I want bravery for the warfare of life," he said.

Richmond and I escorted Burns back to Mrs. Carfrae's, dodging the dirty luggies that were being tossed from upper floor windows. The cry of 'gardyloo' was heard the length of the High Street while I ruminated on an extraordinary creature. As he put it, one never knew whether one was setting sail on the trade winds of wisdom or the mad tornadoes of chaos.

CHAPTER XII

In a cruel twist of fate for the Lord Moray—but a positive stroke of good fortune for me—his lordship's horse demurred at the prospect of heaving his ample frame over a small Highland burn. The stubborn mare stopped short but his lordship did not, the consequence being he was recovering in his northern fastness with a broken collarbone.

This left the lovely Miss Alexander and her friend Miss Ruthven at a rather loose end. They were kept in a modest style to be available to entertain his lordship and his friends at the shortest of notice. In his absence, they were free to follow their own diversions. I took to calling round one evening, where matters took a predictable course with fair Peggy. But it emerged our intimacy quickly went beyond the carnal. She was clear that she was making her way in the world in the only way left open to her, and as soon as she'd be able to accumulate sufficient capital, she would resume her place in respectable society by taking up her trade in cloths and silks.

Her language was most unladylike whenever she referred to her lordship, but her real bile was reserved for the man who had robbed her.

"Do you know the Latin motto of Scotland?" she asked me one evening as we lay on her bed. I shook my head, struggling to recall my brief brush with the classics. "Nemo me impune lacessit—no one provokes me with impunity."

"You have the Latin?"

"Enough to remember that. When I am in a position to take my revenge on the man who reduced me to role of common whore to a half-wit, he will wish he was facing Satan's three faces in the ninth circle of Hell."

It became apparent that Peggy had owned a thriving dressmaking business and had ordered eight bolts of silk through Inglis and Horner, the silk merchants at Mercat Cross. But while she controlled her destiny, she did not command her fate, and it was her fate to have her entire inventory on the premises of Inglis and Horner the night hundreds of pounds of stock disappeared in a robbery.

"But I have a sense who ruined me, and I will pay him back doubly," she said before changing the subject.

By coincidence, the subject of daring robberies was raised by David Balfour in the sedate offices of Samuel Mitchelson, WS, the very next morning.

"It's the damnedest thing," he said. "Old widow Macfarlane, who was to invest that £1,000 with the council, was robbed in the middle of the night. All her jewelry and a substantial number of guinea notes she kept in the house were taken. Yet there was no sign of a break-in—almost as if the thieves had their own key to the place. The damnedest thing," he repeated.

He showed me the newspaper, *The Courant*, which pointed out there had been a string of similar robberies in recent months and there was a £100 reward being offered.

I mentioned it to Peggy that night, and she looked at me quixotically before appearing to decide on a course of action. "I have come to trust you, John Bruce, so I will share this with you, but be warned, it may be dangerous information. Have you seen me talking to a young caddie, Jamie?"

The caddies were everywhere in Edinburgh, carrying letters, delivering messages and trading gossip. One young Highlander seemed to have a particular softness for Peggy. I nodded.

"He looks out for me, checks that I'm not being troubled by drunkards," she said. "He knows my story, and he hears things. He said he also looks out for Annie Johnson, a plump young hussy who works Barefoot Park. One night she was with a drunken Englishman called John Brown. He was bragging about how he could make her look like a real lady in some new silks he'd come into. He joked that he might soon have some jewels too. And the next night John Tapp's shop was robbed of 18 guinea notes, a silver watch and some gold rings.

"Evidently Annie said she met Brown again, and he brought her some white satin—I'd wager the very same that I ordered from London. Brown didn't deny to her that the satin was stolen. In fact, he boasted about how shocked she'd be if she knew the identity of his accomplices in the adventure.

"Well our young caddie Jamie knows well with whom John Brown associates. Brown is never out of Clark's in Fleshmarket Close, where he plays dice and drinks punch with a grocer called Smith, another man called Ainslie and Deacon Brodie, the cabinetmaker."

At Brodie's name, I sat bolt upright. "Old Mrs. Macfarlane had some business with the deacon as part of the investment," I said to Peggy. "They say there was no sign of a breaking and entering, as if the thief had their own key."

Peggy twirled her long blond hair around her finger and sucked in her cheeks, lost in thought.

"Maybe they did," she said. "Jamie says George Smith, the grocer, is known to be a locksmith. He could easily take the impression of a key and make a duplicate copy if they had access to the original."

The suggestion was shocking. The very thought that one of the city's protectors by day was robbing its citizens blind by night was a scandal of historic proportions. Books would be written about it if it ever became public.

"Well it would damage the deacon's reputation if it were known he haunts a night house like Clark's, far less that he spends his evenings fleecing the good citizens of the city where he is a trusted councillor. The question is, what to do with the information now we have it?"

CHAPTER XIII

I saw little of the poet in those early weeks of the new year, in part because of my preoccupation with the winsome Peggy Alexander, in part because Burns had become embroiled in an affair of the heart with a pretty Lothian farmer's daughter he met at a dance in Leith. His tinder heart had been rekindled by the farmer's daughter, yet Meg Cameron was still trooping the colour, most often finding Burns as erect as a grenadier.

One bright Saturday, he suggested to me that we take a walk to Roslin, site of a battle during the Scottish Wars of Independence in which Burns was much interested. It was home to an old ruined castle and the equally dilapidated 15th century Rosslyn Chapel. We set off early and walked down the rocky, wooded bank of the River Esk in silence for a couple of hours. In due course, the sun broke through, and we had the makings of a grand Scottish early spring day. We found the ancient castle overlooking a wooded glen, and the poet wandered around in a daze.

"You know it's a wonder this castle exists even in this ruined state. It was burned by Henry the Eighth during the Rough Wooing, then rebuilt, then fired upon again by Cromwell's troops," said Burns. "It vexes me that we are party to a union that seems to me to boast few advantages but has annihilated a proud independence." It was a recurring complaint of his—that Englishmen who had never been south of the River Tweed populated the drawing rooms of Edinburgh.

Nonetheless, the visit seemed to energize him, and he vowed to devote more of his time experiencing his nation's story at first hand. We sat in the sun, and the conversation inevitably turned to the fairer sex.

"My breast has been widowed these last few months," he said. "I'm not sure what ails me."

I grimaced. "Don't take this the wrong way, Rob, but I think you need three women at any given time: a country girl to mother your offspring, a refined and accomplished lady to act as a friend and companion, and a clean-limbed, low-born lass to satisfy your riotous passions."

He rubbed his brow and smiled. "Aye, you may be right on that, John. My heart has so often been on fire, I believe it is absolutely vitrified. I look upon the fair sex with something like the admiration with which I regard the starry sky on a frosty December night. But I have yet to find all three of the qualities you describe in one package. Jean Armour was the closest, and it may well be that I have to settle on two of three and reflect on it as a fair purse."

He explained that Edinburgh could only be an interlude in his life. "I have many intimacies and friendships here, but I'm afraid they are all of too tender a construction to bear carriage 150 miles. All but you and Richmond," he said softly.

His mind was set on a return to farming. "I do not intend to give up poetry, but being bred to labour secures my independence."

We sat for a while in silence, each reflecting on our lot, before setting back for Edinburgh. We stopped in a local inn for tea, eggs and whisky. The landlady, a talkative woman called Mrs. Wilson, made such a fuss of the bard that when the bill came, he scribbled a verse at the bottom:

> "*My blessing on ye, honest wife!*
> *I ne'er was here before;*
> *Ye've wealth of gear for spoon and knife—*
> *Heart could not wish for more.*"

It maybe wasn't his finest verse, but you wouldn't have separated that goodwife from that scrap of paper for all the tea in the Orient.

CHAPTER XIV

By mid-April, the second edition of the poet's work was heading to the presses. He had spent much of the preceding months in Smellie's shop reading proofs. Three thousand copies were printed and subscriptions were in great demand—the Duke of Argyle signed up for one, and Adam Smith, the brilliant mind from Kirkcaldy, purchased four. Creech, that strange and vain man, promised Burns 100 guineas for the copyright, payment vowed to take place at some future, undisclosed date.

I have to confess there was little in the new edition that excited me—Burns had penned little of worth to augment the raw genius of the Kilmarnock Edition.

Perhaps it was the lack of feminine attachment in the capital that deprived him of his muse, though I enjoyed the inclusion of Address To A Haggis, which was previewed at a gathering of the Crochallan Fencibles. To Burns, the haggis was honest and sonsie, two of the highest compliments he could pay anyone or anything.

The poet, liberated for once by having funds—or at least a promissory note—at hand, decided he would spend some time seeing his country at close quarters. He asked me to accompany him, but since both Richmond and I were committed to our respective employers, he decided to head to the Borders by himself on a new mare he christened Jenny Geddes, after the famously spirited Presbyterian woman who threw a stool at the cleric in St. Giles.

He wrote from Jedburgh to say he was 'a point and a half from being damnably in love' with some doctor's daughter. "I got hold of Miss Lindsay's arm," he said, "and my heart thawed into melting pleasure after being so long frozen up in the Greenland Bay of indifference, amid the noise and nonsense of Edinburgh."

But his amorous ambitions were thwarted after he was warned off by her maiden aunt. "The old, ugly slanderous hag. Hear me O'Heaven and give ear O'Earth—may the burden of antiquated virginity crush her down to the lowest region of the bottomless pit!"

In Duns, he stopped with a local family and attended a church service. "I noticed the young lady of the house attentive but agitated at the sermon dwelling on hellfire," he wrote. "I took her Bible and inscribed:

'Fair maid, you need not take the hint,
Nor idle texts pursue:
'Twas guilty sinners that he meant
Not angels such as you.'"

In his absence I became even more wrapped up in my Peggy. Though Lord Moray had returned to Edinburgh, he had not yet resumed his rakery.

It gave Peggy and me time to discuss how we might foil the felonious talents of Deacon Brodie and his accomplices.

Peggy had uncovered one more delicious morsel of information—John Brown was an alias. She had visited Annie Johnson who, decked in a fine white satin dress, boasted of her Humphrey.

"You'd have thought she'd married the provost, not cuckolded a thief," growled Peggy. "His real name is Humphrey, Humphrey Moore."

It took me some time making inquiries through the good offices of Samuel Mitchelson, but finally word came through from London that a Humphrey Moore had been convicted of theft at the Old Bailey three years prior and sentenced to transportation beyond the seas for a period of seven years. It was apparent that he'd somehow escaped Botany Bay and was now using his villainous talents in Auld Reekie.

"We should report Moore to the Old Town Guard," said Peggy.

"We could. But that wouldn't get your silks back," I said. "And Deacon Brodie would continue his double character unmolested. Even if Moore were to try to spread bad fortune Brodie's way, no one would believe him after he'd been chased down and arrested. No, we need to be cannier than that. What if Moore could be induced to come forward and turn informer?" I suggested.

"And why would he do that?"

I had been thinking on this and had consulted a weighty legal tome on the subject earlier that day.

"A fat reward and the prospect of a pardon. It will go hard enough for him if he is arrested for the robberies in Edinburgh, not to mention his previous depredations. But he would enjoy immunity for all his past performances if a pardon is granted. The public prosecutor would have to obtain a pardon for all offences to allow his evidence against his fellows to be admissible."

It was a suggestion that was to have far-reaching consequences in Edinburgh, a town of uncommon talent where it was said if you stood at the Mercat Cross with a pistol, you could hit 50 geniuses, 50 bankers, 50 lawyers and 50 rogues at any given hour. I mulled how to approach Moore and decided it might be best to wait for him to make the next move.

My mind was distracted from the nefarious Deacon Brodie by a much-distressed Meg Cameron, who happened to visit at Peggy Alexander's one evening. It emerged that Burns had not been entirely jesting on the occasion he said he was the greatest fool when women were the presiding stars—nor when he had mentioned he honoured his king by begetting him loyal subjects. Meg was pregnant with the poet's child, and she asked me for a forwarding address for Burns as she'd been advised to issue him with a writ.

I sent word to Dumfries, where Burns had told me he was heading to take measure of Patrick Miller's farm on the River Nith. A few days later I received a packet from him begging me to send for Meg. "Give the wench 10 or 12 shillings," he said, "but don't for Heaven's sake meddle with her as a piece. You may not like the business, but I tax your friendship thus far."

He was right. I didn't like the business. It suggested to me, whatever purple sentiments he expressed during the quest, he could be cold as Mars once the quarry was snared. But I did his bidding, and the pitiable figure left with her coin, a mere shadow of the red-haired vixen who had bedazzled the poet at the Wig Club. I heard little more of her than she left Edinburgh to marry a Highland cattle drover. I never did find out if she ever had Burns' nestling. More tellingly, neither did he.

CHAPTER XV

The poet's pilgrimage extended through the summer. After taking a look at Miller's farm at Ellisland near Dumfries, he headed back to his native Ayrshire but was not taken with his old neighbourhood.

"He says not one new thing under the sun has happened since he left," Richmond told me, after receiving a letter. "Some embittering recollections have persuaded him he'd be happier anywhere but in Mauchline. You can be sure he's bounced Jean Armour all over the district—she holds a strange witchcraft over him—and her ogre of a father is likely still trying to have him thrown in jail."

Richmond was more prophetic than he could know. Burns had indeed rekindled his romance with Jean, as was to become readily apparent to all nine months later. The man was as fecund as the spring. His life was a shambles, yet he was still a slave to fancy and whim.

He returned briefly to Edinburgh where he moved to lodge with Willie Nicol further down the Royal Mile. But he was itching to continue his tour northward, perhaps disconcerted by the Meg Cameron affair and her potential claim on him. I found him one evening sitting alone with a bottle in Johnnie Dowie's tavern.

"I have taken refuge with a friend who has more of the milk of human kindness than the entire human race put together—a friend to the friendless, a universal philanthropist, and his name is a beloved bottle of good old port," he said.

Even then he had not settled his mind on farming. "It's the only thing of which I know anything, and Heaven above knows but little do I understand even of that." He mentioned again his desire to head to Jamaica or even perhaps try for a career in the excise if he could secure the patronage of Robert Graham of Fintry, an Excise Board Commissioner who was also a subscriber to the poet's Edinburgh Edition.

The Meg Cameron business, the problems with Jean, an ailing child in Ayrshire, uncertainty about his career choice and an inability to get any money out of Creech had revived his blue devils.

He took off almost immediately with the curmudgeonly schoolmaster, Nicol, heading for Argyll. He sent a package from the head of Loch Long, which he described as 'a country where savage streams tumble over savage mountains, thinly overspread with savage flocks, which starvingly support its savage inhabitants.'

He complained that his Highland tour was marred by Nicol, 'the obstinate son of Latin prose,' but he absorbed the old Scots stories and they poured out of him in lines that he set to ancient songs picked up from musicians like the celebrated fiddler Niel Gow whom he met in Dunkeld.

By the time he was ready to head south, he'd had about all he could tolerate of the irascible Nicol, who had determined he was heading straight back to Auld Reekie rather than meandering through Perthshire and the Ochil Hills. Burns wrote me and wanted to meet in Stirling.

I had my own reasons for wishing to escape the capital. Not only was Lord Moray back in the saddle in the room above my head, but Peggy was late, with the chances being more than probable that any hatchling was mine. I was much taken with Peggy and determined to help her get her silks back, but I was forced to admit she was better equipped for saturnalia than the sacrament.

I made up some story for Balfour about a family crisis and headed toward Stirling on a borrowed pony. I met the poet in a modest inn the next day, and we wandered up to the castle—a less imposing version of Edinburgh's own fortress—only to find the Great Hall had fallen into disrepair. This sent Burns into a rage about the depredations of Scotland's proud history at the hands of the House of Hanover. "Swift had it right. We should burn everything English but their coal," he said.

When we returned to our inn, we encountered an elderly Jacobite landlady, a Mrs. Bruce, who claimed direct descent from Robert the Bruce. Not only that, she said she possessed the Bruce's helmet and two-handed sword. She brought the weapon out of an old trunk. It certainly looked of a vintage to be nearly 500 years old, but there was no way of knowing its true providence. It was enough for Burns, though—he fell on his knees before her and beckoned her to confer a knighthood on us both.

Later, he took out a diamond stylus he kept on his person and began to engrave a windowpane. When he was finished, he sat back to admire his handiwork. It read:

'The injured Stuart line is gone,
A race outlandish fills their throne;
An idiot race, to honour lost;
Who know them best, despise them most.'

"Rab, do you really think publicly expressing such strongly Jacobite sympathies is a wise course of action in such nervous days?" I asked. "If it became known, it would hardly bode well for your career in the employ of His Majesty's Excise."

"You may have a point there, John. But too late now. I will brave misfortune and ruin and claim an uncommon attachment to the British Constitution if I am ever found out."

Talk turned to my domestic vexations, and he raised his bumper. "Welcome to the venerable society of fathers, my friend."

"I hope that it is many years before I take my seat at that august gathering," I said disconsolately. I had seen the chaos that having a child out of wedlock could cause and had no wish to bring any poor cub into that world.

The next day we headed back to Edinburgh through Fife. We stopped at Dunfermline Abbey where Burns took to the pulpit and admonished me in mock tones for my fornication. "You are a sinner, John Bruce. Your amorous gropings may be like the great African ape learning to play one of Stradivari's famed instruments. But you are a sinner, and you must sit on the stool of repentance."

His performance came to an inglorious end. A minister with a face like grey slate had interrupted our revelry.

As we were leaving, he knelt and kissed two broad flagstones that were rumoured to mark the grave of the Bruce. Once more, he cursed the neglect of Scotland's heroes.

CHAPTER XVI

Our return to Edinburgh saw the commencement of a series of events that created a great schism in our friendship. The passage of years has helped me appreciate Burns was as much a cork dancing along on the torrent of emotion as I was. Perhaps because he was older, and I revered him, I expected him to be wiser—more able to resist the passions and instincts that cause so much pain. But for all he maintained he was a man of conscience who acted an honest part among his fellow creatures, he was at the mercy of those passions, and his conscience was often left flapping in the wind.

The rupture in our relations had a name, Clarinda. That was not her real name; she was Agnes McLehose. But she became her pen name, Clarinda, to Burns and me as I ferried letters between the two, facilitating his seduction as he sought his Holy Grail—a refined woman who would satisfy his riotous passions.

But I'm getting ahead of myself. On our return to Edinburgh, Burns took up rooms overlooking St. Andrew's Square, bordering the New Town, but life was quickly thrown into disarray once again. In late October, he received word from Ayrshire that his daughter had died.

He sent me a note to say he was a girl out of pocket, but when I met up with him in Johnnie Dowie's tavern, any sense of stoicism had left him.

The little girl had been living with Jean, now four months pregnant with the next set of Burns' progeny, and had fallen foul of some kind of accident. The poet was incoherent with anger, pain and grief, dulled by pints of wine. He said only that she had died by careless, murdering mischance.

"My life reminds me of a ruined temple: What strength, what proportion in some parts! What unsightly gaps, what prostrate ruins in others!" he said ruefully.

With his future firmly in the West—either in Dumfries or back in Ayrshire in partnership on the family farm with his brother Gilbert—the poet's time in Edinburgh seemed to be almost done.

Then, a chance encounter at a tea party with a pert 29-year-old Clarinda intervened. She happened to flash the poet a smile, which he felt in the pocket of his breeches, and the experience left him like a man with a head of wax who has wandered too long in the sun.

It was a bitter early December evening when he exploded into Johnnie Dowie's. "Almighty love reigns and revels in my bosom," he proclaimed loudly. "I'm ready to hang myself for a young Edinburgh widow."

He knew little of her beyond what he could prise from her in the genteel surroundings of Miss Erskine Nimmo's drawing room—namely that her name was Agnes McLehose and that she had been married, had a brood of children and lived at Generals Entry just off Potterrow. "She has invited me to tea two days hence, and I am already thinking of revising my plan to leave

Edinburgh for good. You know me; my whims carry me farther than boasted reason ever did a philosopher."

I was dubious about the future prospects built on such a tenuous acquaintance, but I was happy to see my friend's spirits revived after such trying news of late. When he asked me to use my legal connections to find all I could about Miss McLehose, I agreed gladly. And when we parted, and he climbed aboard a coach to take him to his new lodgings, I reflected that he seemed to have rediscovered some of the strange magic that possessed him when first we met. For Burns, love truly was the alpha and omega of human existence.

The news the next day blew ill for all concerned. Burns sent me a note to say he was at that moment being tended to by Lang Sandy Wood, after falling from his coach on the way home. The prognosis was likely dislocation of the knee, which was going to require a month of enforced idleness.

I visited the new lodgings at St. James Square to find him prostate with his leg elevated on a cushion. "Curse the clumsiness of a drunken coachman," he spat.

"You were scarcely a paragon of sobriety," I pointed out.

I apprised him of what I'd found out about Agnes. Through a lawyer who had known her husband, I discovered she was the daughter of a well-known Glasgow surgeon, Andrew Craig, and had married young to a lawyer, James McLehose, with whom she had four children. He had treated her shabbily, and they had separated, after which he served time in a debtors' prison in London. But, crucially, he was still alive, so she was not a widow and was still married in the eyes of the law.

"Surely, it's early days to be considering matrimony in any case?" I reasoned.

"Perhaps," he conceded. "But I am strangely taken with her. And I'm not often mistaken.

"Yet I'm now a poet on stilts. Since I can't woo her in person, I will have to bring her down with some poetic lines. It's as well that I'm an old hawk at the sport. I'm going to ask your indulgence once again, John. If she is indeed still married, I suspect she will not welcome regular mail from a prospective suitor. Are you willing to be interlocutor in this game of hearts?"

Would that I had said no.

CHAPTER XVII

Perhaps it was the isolation of the enforced confinement to his quarters that produced the madness that ensued—lack of physical activity, lack of interaction with the natural world, lack of touch.

Whatever it was, a kind of delirium took hold of Burns. And it proved contagious. Agnes became as enraptured as the poet.

Burns explained that she lived on an annuity paid by her cousin William Craig, a lonely Calvinist whose goal in life was to protect the chastity and reputation of the fair Mrs. McLehose. Stealth had to be the operative word if, in his words, 'The bird is to be brought from her aerial towerings down to my foot.'

He did not believe that the regular Edinburgh Penny Post could be trusted, or more particularly he was worried that his letters might be intercepted by Craig once delivered. The solution was to have me drop off his missives to her servant girl by hand.

She had sent him an invitation to tea, and he begged me to convey his apologies and explain his circumstances. He handed me a letter that was not yet sealed. "The secret is to present her with a cool, deliberate, prudent reply that hints at unnamed feelings," he said.

I slipped the note from its envelope. "You are one of the first of lovely form and noble mind," it read. "I do love you still better for having so fine a taste and turn for poetry."

Burns must've seen something in my expression for he waved a dismissive hand. "You may," he said, "change the word love so I speak of esteem or respect or any other tame expression you please in its place."

The letter continued on in similar vacuous form and seemed to me transparently superficial. But then I was a mere fledgling in the art of erotic falconry. I took the letter and trudged up the new bridge toward Agnes McLehose's small flat on Potterrow.

The door was opened by a pretty young servant with a port wine birthmark that covered her left cheek and ran down her neck. I asked to speak to her mistress and she begged me to wait inside. It was a matter of moments before a delicate woman of perhaps 30 years rushed to greet me.

"Mr. Bruce, I gather you are an emissary from the bard," she said. "Please come in and join me for tea."

I gathered that I was considered no threat to her reputation, which was strangely disappointing since she was very alluring, and I could see why Burns had become so besotted with her. She was exceedingly petite—with small hands and feet, good teeth, a soft voice, a coquettish, upturned nose and voluptuous bosom. She excited, whether she intended to or not, what Dr. Johnson would have called amorous propensities.

She read the letter Burns had sent, then sat at a writing desk, scribbling some lines of reply. She had already compiled a packet bulging with paper.

"If I were his sister, I would call on him to see how his leg is. But 'tis a censorious world, so I will have to resign myself to sending him my best wishes and some poetry of mine he had asked to read. Could you please convey them to him?" she asked as she handed me the packet. With that, she rang a bell and the servant reappeared.

"Jenny, could you see Mr. Bruce to the door," she demanded.

I was dismissed like a glorified caddie, though the smile I received from the servant as I left Potterrow was almost worth the trip.

Burns perked up considerably when I arrived back at his perch at St. James Square. He ripped open the packet and chuckled as he read its contents. "Listen to this, Bruce, my lad, 'We are indeed strangers in one sense but of near kin in many respects. Your lines were truly poetic—give me all you can spare.'"

He paused briefly and then looked at me with a knowing grin. "You see, my friend? Prudence must rule when in pursuit of women; only vague suggestion of nameless feeling will yield a hungry heart."

I was forced to smile, too, but I felt a sense of deep foreboding about this assignation, as if we were all sitting in a carriage where the horses have been spooked and bolted, while the driver has saved himself by leaping off. Everyone involved in this little vignette was out of control.

CHAPTER XVIII

I was brought back from the exotic world of Venus to the mundane savagery of Mars by yet another robbery, this time of the ceremonial silver mace from the university wrenched from its bed of blue velvet in the middle of the night by persons unknown.

The citizens of Edinburgh could talk of little else. My landlady, Mrs. Carfrae, viewed it a divine augury of the city's moral and physical decline—a judgment on the capital's dissolute ways. "Hanging is too good for the likes of these villains," she prattled over breakfast as I read out the news.

I had been avoiding Peggy Alexander, as if forestalling the conversation would make the prospect of her pregnancy disappear with the light dusting of snow we'd had that morning. But the robbery had persuaded me the moment was right to help Peggy win back her silks and get her out from under the patronage of my Lord Moray.

I mulled the best course of action as I emerged from Baxter's Close on my way to the good offices of Samuel Mitchelson, WS, only to see a dandyish- looking figure wearing a new dark blue jacket, a fashionable waistcoat, black satin breeches and white satin stockings while swaggering out from Brodie's Close on the opposite side of the High Street. It was the deacon himself, hair fully dressed, and in good humour as he hailed his fellow burghers and made his way toward me.

I must have cut a strange figure, mouth agape at the man's audacity. He was every inch the upstanding stalwart of the city's establishment—an elegant gentleman whose family name stood above the close where he lived. Yet, I had no doubts that hours earlier he'd had those fine hands around the hollow crowns of the university's silver mace.

He strolled up to me, bowed his head and gave an unctuous smile. "How do things stand with you, Mr. Bruce? I haven't seen you since you fled Lord Moray's Wig Club with the poet. I see they're calling Burns Scotland's bard now. But then titles come and go. Caligula raised his favourite horse to a senator, after all." He gave a low chuckle, baring his teeth before continuing on his theme.

"Maybe the attractions of the posture girls were not to the taste of Mr. Burns? Perhaps he relishes contrary sensations?" he said.

This time it was me that was forced to laugh. No one was less inclined to such sensations than the poet.

"I fear you are much mistaken about Mr. Burns, sir," I said. "But I find that you never really know a man until you have done business with him. On another matter entirely, do you recall old widow Macfarlane? You were kind enough to help her out with some bargain carpentry. By strange coincidence, she was robbed a few days later, and the uncanny thing was there was no sign of a break-in, as if the culprits had their own keys. Awful strange, don't you think?"

The deacon, who had been so full of pomp just seconds earlier, glowered at me under darkening brows. "You have a sharp tongue, sir," he said. "Be careful it doesn't cut your throat." And with that, he was off up the High Street like a trout up a stream.

I was conscious I had just made a dangerous enemy, so I sent a note to Peggy through the young Highland caddie, Jamie, asking her to make an excuse to steal away from Lord Moray's service that night.

We met in the back room at the Fortune's Tavern, up Stamp Office Close. It was a foul night and the hostelry was all but empty. I ranged beside a blazing fire waiting for Peggy to appear. The logs on the fire spat and crackled like sausages in a pan. I reflected my predicament was not unlike a well-fired sausage, singed to a crisp after veering too close to the fleshly flame.

Peggy entered, and the conversation at the next table stopped as the two gentlemen sitting there took in the sight of the comely blond lass, gloriously attired in the brown riding outfit with hooped dress and bonnet. She stopped to have a word with the host, letting the gathering know that she was familiar with the place, and my neighbours went back to their claret.

I must have presented a pale, ghostly countenance. "Dear God, John Bruce. What ails you?" she asked breezily.

I didn't know what to say. The last time I'd seen her, she looked the same deathly shade as me, as she fretted aloud about the prospect of being with child. Since then, I had kept my distance—it was clear neither of us was intent on finishing what we had started.

She divined my concern, took my hand and gazed into my eyes with that disconcerting squint of hers. "John, don't fret. I was late, so I took a purgative of turpentine. I'm not with child, so you can let the blood flow to your head again. I should have told you sooner, but you have been more elusive than the Young Pretender."

It was a curious sensation to be flooded with relief, mixed with a trace of regret that I had behaved in such an unmanly fashion. I resolved I would make it up to her.

"Did you hear about the robbery at the university?" I asked, eager to change the subject. She nodded—of course she had. The rumour had galloped up and down the Royal Mile before the bells of St. Giles' had struck six in the forenoon.

"I think it's time we put our plan in place," I said, fleshing out the idea to win her consent. I stuck firmly to the idea that we could not just blurt out our suspicions about Brodie lest they reach his ears and place us both in danger. The key was in persuading John Brown to break with his villainous accomplices.

We sought out Archibald Cockburn, the city's sheriff-depute, who lived on the second floor of a neighbouring wynd—one of the few more affluent citizens who had not yet emigrated to the New Town. He was related by marriage to the powerful Dundas family and was reputed widely to be incorruptible.

After explaining to his servant the urgent nature of our business, we were shown into an oak-panelled study that was lit by beeswax candles, and then joined promptly by a slow-moving, bull of a man in his late middle age—the senior judge in Midlothian.

Cockburn said he'd just sat down to dinner, but the prospect of an advance in the case was worth his broth going cold. "These insidious plunderers have baffled all possibility of detection, so what makes a young law clerk think he can bring them to justice?" he asked forcefully.

"If your Lordship would permit, my...client here, Miss Alexander, was the victim of these depraved individuals when her bolts of silk were taken from Inglis and Horner. She has since gleaned certain information that suggests a new tactic that might be used to break the combination of men leagued together against our society."

Cockburn perched his spectacles on his mottled nose and took a long look at Peggy for the first time. "You look familiar, young lady. Do I know you?"

The former posture girl blushed, which I had never seen before, and smiled demurely. "I shouldn't have thought so, your Lordship. I'm very new to the capital."

Cockburn was too long in the tooth to fall for fluttering eyelashes, but he decided to let it rest. "Be that as it may, what is this information. And what makes you think there is a combination of individuals?"

"We have very few specifics, your Lordship, beyond the certain knowledge that one of the men in question was sentenced to seven years in Botany Bay at the Old Bailey, but he escaped and fled north," I explained.

"Go on," said Cockburn, whose keen legal mind was already whirring.

"The government has offered a reward for the capture of these dastardly felons, to no effect," I continued. "But what if a pardon was added to sweeten the pot? The runaway thief might look more favourably on the prospect of offering up his accomplices if it prospered him so. If he is caught now, he'll hang for sure."

Cockburn was nodding in agreement. "So you came to me in the belief I could use my government connections to secure His Majesty's Pardon?

And that's all you know of the matter?"

"There are some suspicions, your Lordship, but no evidence that could justify tearing a man from the bosom of society to answer for his alleged vices," I said.

Cockburn looked at me in queer fashion, plainly aware I knew more than I was letting on. But he was satisfied for now. He'd been around the courts enough to know the restraints of conscience and honour among criminals are not tightly bound.

"One more thing, your Lordship, Miss Alexander is not seeking a reward for her help, but should these villains be apprehended, will she be entitled to retrieve the value of her plundered stock?"

He leaned in close to Peggy and spoke with deliberation. "If your actions help end these depredations, I will make sure you have enough silk to clothe every lady at the next Caledonian Hunt Ball. And I'll throw in Lord Moray's flea-ridden old wig as a gratuity."

With that, he rose and retired to finish his broth.

CHAPTER XIX

I regaled the poet with the whole story. At the mention of Brodie's name, I expected a gasp of stupefaction, but I was disappointed. "I told you the deacon was not all he seemed," was all Burns said, deadpan.

He pointed out a flaw in my plan. "This gang of thieves has been successful thus far," he said. "The amount they have raked in far exceeds the paltry reward on offer. For your plan to work, they must strike again—and they must fail."

He had a point. Why would Brown break with Brodie, if there was no prospect of discovery? Burns, with his leg still resting on an elevated cushion, said he would think on it.

"Meanwhile, I would further beg your indulgence to transport this missive to Mrs. McLehose," he said. "She was brought into this world as Agnes, folk call her Nancy, but from now on to me she will be Clarinda, and I will be Sylvander, just in case the letters fall into the hands of her inquisitive cousin. She says she will feel less restrained if we use pen names. The letter is there on the table. Take a read."

I did so, almost overcome by its impudence. There was much talk about 'the tender witchcraft of love' being added to 'the honourable sentiments of manly friendship,' to which only one more 'delightful morsel' could be added to create the most delicious composition of all, 'like adding cream to strawberries'.

It was not the poet's most subtle attempt at seduction, but I merely nodded my connivance.

I gazed out of the window of Burns' garret, watching those in a gathering throng on the street greet one another and oft times take a proffered drink. I had almost forgotten it was New Year's Eve.

The Church of Scotland had used whatever fading influence it had left to discourage the celebration of Christmas as too popish, but it could do nothing about festivities to celebrate the pagan Hogmanay, the end of the old year and a recognition of the winter solstice. Across Scotland the redding—a cleaning out of the ashes in the house and the paying of debts—cleared the way for a new year launched by luck, joy and a break with the past.

"It will be a quiet Hogmanay for you this year," I said.

"Ah yes, quiet. Very quiet," replied Burns. "There's plenty of time for revels. By chance, this damned knee has given me time to repair and tinker with a new work for Jamie Johnson's Scots Musical Museum. It was good advice to collect all the scattered verses from across the country, and I think this is one that is exceedingly expressive. It's an old song called Auld Lang Syne, and it has never been in print, nor even in manuscript, until I took it down from an old man."

I brought it over to the window and read it twice. "It reeks of Scotland, but its message is universal," I noted.

"Just so, John. This is my true métier, I believe—making the songs of a people. Scotland is full of writers, but there is no Scottish culture. We are in thrall to the French and the English. My way is this: I consider the poetic sentiment to match the musical expression then look for objects in nature around me that are in harmony with my cogitations. This cursed knee and this solitary fireside have afforded me time to commit some of my effusions to paper. What do you think?"

I read it with a warm glow, marvelling at its simplicity yet near perfect sentiment for the turning of the year. "I think it's time we had a cup of kindness before I go and deliver your package," I said.

CHAPTER XX

After our next meeting, I reflected the lack of stimulation seemed to have provoked the poet to take leave of his senses altogether.

He arranged to meet me two days later in John's Coffee House on Parliament Square, arriving with some difficulty in a hired sedan chair. It was a dreary, windswept occasion marked by most of the capital's recovering denizens in their beds or round their hearths.

John's was known for being popular with opponents of the Union, and loud doggerel verse against that infamous marriage of convenience was at the ready.

I had just come from Clarinda's home on Potterrow where the pretty servant girl with the port wine birthmark, Jenny Clow, had passed on her mistress' response to Burns' latest letter. Clarinda was in the country, visiting relatives, which allowed Jenny to be free with her tongue. It's said that no man is a hero to his valet—equally then, no woman is revered by her handmaiden.

"The mistress is all aflutter," said Jenny. "Read it if you don't believe me."

She handed me the open letter, and I couldn't resist. The prose was light as tinsel: "I'm looking for a friend who might love me with tenderness, unmixed with selfishness, who could be my friend, companion, protector...now Heaven has, I hope, sent me this blessing in my Sylvander."

"It's so syrupy, it would make you spew," giggled Jenny.

It was naïve and winsome, no doubt, but its author wrote from the heart, and so she found her target in the heart. I was forced to surrender by its charm, and it wasn't even aimed at me.

"They're both as giddy as seasick goats," was all I could manage in reply.

"It's fleshy lust that drives them both to madness," said Jenny, leaning in so close I could smell the herbs in her soap. "But he'll be sorely disappointed. She may tease that she could be an enthusiast in fun, but she's too pious for your poet. She's more feared of hellfire than devoted to rapture. He'll be lucky if he sees her petticoat." She winked at me with a leer that suggested she herself would willingly entertain a company of grenadiers. For a second, it was me who was giddy as a goat.

I grabbed the packet and headed for the coffee shop. Burns consumed it avidly. Among its contents was a silhouette portrait of Clarinda. He was well pleased. "I am going to take this to the goldsmith across the square, and ask him to set it as a miniature in a locket. It is a pledge of love and perhaps a prelude to matrimony," he said.

I was at a loss for words, on the cusp of pointing out that this was a woman he had met just once. Instead, I inquired whether he had enjoyed a tolerable Hogmanay.

"I have a confession on that front, John. I did not share this with you because I know your tender feelings on the matter. But after you left my rooms, I struck out for a Jacobite dinner on the anniversary of the king over the water's birthday—a day as hallowed as the ceremonies of religion and sacred to the memory of the suffering of my king and my forefathers."

I was astonished. "Burns, your forefathers were likely as hostile to the House of Stuart as mine," I said. "They were motivated by power and religion, not by love of Scotland. They may not transport Jacobites to the colonies any longer, but it is still a dangerous business to sympathize openly with a Stuart restoration. Didn't you mention that you have revived your interest in becoming an exciseman? How can you possibly work for the Crown and secretly plot its downfall?"

"I am indeed pursuing that line. I have been at pains to solicit the patronage of Robert Graham of Fintry, the excise commissioner whom I met last summer at Blair Atholl. He subscribed to the second impression of my book, and I am appointed to meet with him five days hence," he said.

I threw up my arms. "Then I have nothing to offer you but my confusion," I said.

The bard chuckled and sat back in his chair. "John, I recall the words of the philosopher Lord Bolingbroke in a letter to the writer Swift, wherein he said, 'Adieu dear Swift—with all thy faults, I love thee entirely. Make an effort to love me with all mine.' It is a glorious sentiment, without which there can be no friendships."

We sat and gazed at the fire, each consumed in thought. He broke the silence. "I want you to meet two gentlemen I spoke to briefly at the dinner—old soldiers who survived the rout at Culloden. I thought you might be interested in their story," he said. "I wager it might be raw, yet rich, poetic material."

Just as St. Giles struck noon, two older gentlemen entered the coffee house and headed in our direction. One was tall and broad, with a single-breasted black coat that had seen better days, a black cocked hat and a large scar down the side of his face. The other was shorter and walked stiffly like someone plagued by rheumatism. He wore a brown wig, a brown hat and had shaggy eyebrows that seemed to be permanently raised in wonder like Gothic arches. They looked like the men of war they had been, as if they'd both lain down to bleed awhile before rising to fight again.

The shorter one sat down and extended his leg with a sigh of relief.

"It's as well The Butcher Cumberland is not still chasing you, Duncan. You're no longer fit to walk let alone fight," said the taller one in a rasping voice. He turned to the poet. "Well Mr. Burns, how goes it with your war wound today?"

"Sir, I prefer the plough to the pistol, but I can scarcely say I'd swagger with either this day. Gentlemen, may I introduce my friend and accomplice in revels, John Bruce of Annan."

I hoped against hope that neither of these old soldiers had been in the Queensberry Arms in my hometown the night my grandfather was abducted by the Jacobite army for expressing his Hanoverian sympathies.

Neither showed a glimmer of recognition.

"John, this is Captain Farquhar MacGillivray of Dalcrombie and Lieutenant Duncan Mackintosh of Drummond, late of Lady Mackintosh's regiment, both of whom escaped death and transportation after the deadly harvest at Culloden."

"A deadly harvest it was," said MacGillivray. "'Tis no wonder nothing grows on that accursed bog to this day. The soil is hardscrabble still because of rotten bones."

The poet begged him to tell his tale. And so he did:

"We were in poor spirits before the battle, but it's a mercy of providence we didn't know how bleak was to be our fate—the death and exile across the oceans of an entire civilization.

"It was a chilly, miserable April morning. We were tired and hungry. We got by on a single biscuit that morning, while the redcoats celebrated the Duke of Cumberland's birthday with two gallons of brandy for each regiment. We were on battle stations the day before, and that night we set off on a 20-mile march with the intent of springing a surprise attack on Cumberland's regiments. It came to naught, and by dawn we heard Cumberland was advancing. The Prince decided we would stand and engage him at Culloden—as ill-fated a decision as was ever made by a commander-in-chief. He in his Glenfinnan buckle brogues had never tried to effect a Highland charge across a soaking bog, so how would he know?

"We waited in that misery until mid-morning. It was raining as sore as I ever saw it, hail and rain and a strong wind in our faces. Their artillery opened up, and still we stood there as grapeshot tore into us, spreading blood and bone and limbs in all direction.

"A madness came upon the men, and when the word was given, we launched a ferocious charge on the government's left flank, following my cousin Alexander MacGillivray. We split through their front line of defence with a brave but rash charge. Alexander and many others fell early, shot through the head and heart by a volley of muskets. By some miracle we two"—he pointed at Mackintosh—"made it unscathed to fight hand to hand with Barrell's 4th Foot. The redcoats had muskets and bayonets, while we were armed with just pistols and broadswords. Nonetheless, the odds were even at close quarters, and they fell in large numbers. But it was too late. The Macdonalds on our left had even further to charge than us and were easy prey for Cumberland's great guns."

Mackintosh took up the tale. "Word came through for our regiment to fall back," he said. "I remember Lachlan Mackintosh, our Lieutenant Colonel, shouting to me that it was all going to pot and that there would be no great succor for us that day.

"Thank God for the Frenchies and exiles of the Royal Ecossais. They covered our retreat and prevented a massacre. And that was it—over in an hour. We fled to Inverness and thankfully avoided the dragoons, as they took no prisoners, instead preferring to slaughter the defeated. From there, we made it to Arisaig and a boat to France where we both spent some years.

"We marched behind some funny folk to be sure," said MacGillivray. "But it is a dagger that remains lodged in my heart—the loss of lands, the exile of family, the ban on the tartan, the oath of allegiance to the Hanoverian usurpers. A greater parcel of rogues never lived."

I looked around, quailing at the prospect this seditious account had been overheard. But the poet sat quietly nodding, seething. "A parcel o' rogues indeed. A parcel o' rogues indeed," he repeated.

CHAPTER XXI

It turned out Burns had done more than just attend the dinner with the sympathizer of the House of Stuart on that December 31. He'd also penned some lines of Jacobite enthusiasm for the Royal Wanderer that were as execrable as they were dangerous. It was as well for all concerned that Charles Edward Stuart died in Rome a month later. Rumours circulated around the country that Burns had been jailed for writing Jacobite verses that maligned the king. Had it not been for the Young Pretender's death, fiction may have turned to fact.

As it was, in the days that followed, the poet's devotions were fully occupied on the coquettish figure fussing around Potterrow, waiting for word from, or better yet sight of, Robert Burns.

Having successfully ventured as far as Parliament Square by sedan chair, Burns had arranged to visit Clarinda soon into the new year and dragged me along, lest the neighbours draw the wrong conclusions from this delicate situation. We arrived just as it was getting dark, so Clarinda need not have worried about the goodwives' tittle-tattle. Jenny Clow showed us in, and I noticed that she smiled flirtatiously at the poet, a look he caught since he gave her a knowing wink as she led us to her mistress. Clarinda appeared and took my breath away. She wore a powder blue, low-cut gown of silk that clung to her body. Yellow silk shoes were stunning, and her hair was piled high on her head. She glided into the room like a magnificent swan, and I fell in love with her.

But she only had eyes for one man.

Burns took her hand, and his lips lingered on her silk glove. "Madam, the man who sees you and does not love deserves to be damned for his stupidity," he said.

She simpered but tried to retain some semblance of propriety. "If I believed your words, I should become vain," she said. "I'm aware that many a glorious woman has been undone by having her head turned. Greetings, Mr. Bruce. Please sit gentlemen."

Jenny appeared with tea served in small porcelain bowls, and the conversation stuttered along until Clarinda asked Burns about his future plans. He admitted he was torn between farming in Dumfries or a career in the excise. While collecting taxes on commodities was no life for a rhymer, he acknowledged life as a gauger had its compensations—namely £50 a year, a pension and a job for life.

"The future, I have said to myself, is still before me, so on reason I build resolve. I have difficulties to encounter, but they are not insuperable," said Burns.

He then dared talk of Jean Armour and his son in Ayrshire. But he said his future was not with her. "I am looking for a lady of native genius, poignant wit, strength of mind, generous sincerity of soul and the sweetest tenderness," he said as he gazed at his Clarinda with those penetrating eyes.

I thought she might melt.

It was at that point I excused myself, claiming some task that had by some supernatural force just been recalled from the depths of memory. Neither protested my departure. Yet when I left the room, Jenny seemed pleased to see me.

"Two's company, three's a crowd, four's too much and five's not allowed, Mr. Bruce," she said with a lascivious laugh. "Why don't you come and wait in my room until Mr. Burns is done with the mistress?"

The web was becoming ever more tangled, and before long it would bind us all.

CHAPTER XXII

It was three days before I saw the poet again to ask how the visit had gone.

I had spent the previous evening with Peggy Alexander, whom I had bumped into at the entrance to Baxter's Close. She was clearly in some distress and invited me to her rooms—not with the wanton enthusiasm of times past but as a friend and confidant. She told me the American War had disrupted Lord Moray's tobacco interests, and he was broken financially.

"I have to find new lodgings and a new source of silver," she said. "I have saved some but not enough to spare me the fate of Annie Johnson and all the other jades down at Barefoot Park. I truly believed I could resume my place in society, but without my silks, it seems I am reduced to a common mercenary," she said quietly with a tear running down one beautiful cheek.

She tried to compose herself but broke down and buried her head in my chest. She looked up and whispered that, to add insult to injury, Brodie had been forced upon her by her patron before he revealed his parlous financial state. "I'm without hope of redemption, and no one can think worse of me than I think of myself," she said.

I tried to comfort her by saying we'd recover her fortune, but I was no closer to a scheme to induce Brodie and his gang to strike again, and there had been no word from Archibald Cockburn, the sheriff-depute, about the offer of pardon.

I was in grey spirits when I later met with Burns, but his mood was flushed with all the bright colours of the rainbow.

"I believe my Clarinda is a gloriously amicable, fine woman, and we are on the cusp of that delicious passion whose most devoted slave I have more than once had the honour of being," he said as we gathered over a bowl in Johnnie Dowie's tavern in Libberton Wynd.

He was also cheered by his meeting with Excise Commissioner Graham of Fintry, whose patronage he needed. "I requested orders for instruction, and I'm in on a list for a vacancy in a division that would offer me the independence so dear to my soul but that has so often been distant from my situation."

"And how will Mrs. McLehose enjoy being the wife of a gauger running around the country testing yeasty barrels?" I wondered aloud.

"You have fairly hit upon the horns of a dilemma, and I confess I do not have an answer," said Burns. "But I am not discouraged. I believe Clarinda's happiness is twisted with the threads of my existence."

He supped deeply, spending some time gazing into the fire. And as one who had slipped into a trance only to startle himself awake, he then clapped his hands loudly.

"By the by, I may have a solution to the problem of the sticky-fingered deacon," he said.

I moved forward to encourage him to explain. And so he did. He had met Graham of Fintry at the General Excise Office for Scotland in an old mansion in Chessel's Court off Canongate, the central collecting point for all taxes and duties in the country. "A body should mention in passing to Brodie about all the bank notes just lying around the place like fallen leaves under a harvest moon," he said.

"Is that true?" I asked, eyes wide.

"Not at all. I didn't see a single shilling while there. But Brodie is a greedy demon who would risk destroying the vine to eat the sweetest grape. If the idea is whispered in his ear, he will try, and chances are he will fail and hang."

CHAPTER XXIII

Burns' idea to lure Brodie to his own demise had merit—and its odds of success improved immeasurably with the news the next day that the reward for information that would lead to the discovery and conviction of robbers had been increased to 20 guineas for each name, and a pardon was being offered to anyone who helped apprehend the guilty parties. Archibald Cockburn had clearly succeeded in twisting the right arms.

But I scarcely had time to plot the next move, given my role as full-time chaperone to Sylvander and Clarinda.

She was alive to what the neighbours might think and the prospect of her cousin discovering the illicit affair, such as it was. At the time, I was under the impression that the only delicious passions being indulged were between me and Jenny Clow. I only discovered later how truly naïve I had been.

The poet visited by sedan chair for the third time, and I sat once more in Clarinda's drawing room like a devoted spaniel fawning over the mistress of the house, even as she neglected me entirely. Yet I saw and heard enough to know that trouble was brewing in paradise. Clarinda seemed intent on turning the conversation toward religion.

"Heaven has not endowed you with such uncommon powers of mind to employ them in the manner you have," she said, causing the poet to scowl. He obviously had not intended to let her see that side of his personality so early in the relationship as he quickly repaired his countenance with a forced grimace.

"I firmly believe that every honest, upright man, of whatever sect, will be accepted by the Deity," he said. And then taking from an old Ayrshire weaver's grace, he added, "'Lord, grant that we may lead a gude life; for a gude life makes a gude end; at least it helps weel!'"

She lapped up this rustic wisdom, reaching over to take his hand. "My God! Sylvander, why am I so anxious to make you embrace the Gospel? I dare not probe too deep for an answer."

Having made contact, the poet was extremely anxious that I retire and admonished me with a nod of his head. Yet for me, even the prospect of a tumble with the maid held little attraction compared to sitting at Clarinda's feet with tongue hanging out and tail wagging.

Despite the auspicious circumstances, it turned out that his carnal ambitions came to naught. "This affair is starting to cause me no end of anguish," he admitted when we met later. "I made the case that when two of nature's noblest productions drink from the same cup of love and bliss, the normal rules of decorum do not apply. Yet she would not relent, claiming secret misgivings that Heaven would not approve because of her situation. She claims I have stolen her soul, but there seems little chance I will prevail in matters more temporal."

As he took a long slug on a mug of claret, he turned and stared into me with those powerful eyes.

All of this happened just one day after he had sounded so optimistic about the future. But he was more perceptive than most. Perhaps he had been given a glimpse of the Promised Land and, like Moses, knew he could never enter. Whatever the reason, Burns was firmly in the grip of the blue devils, and the unbounded exuberance about Clarinda began to ebb.

CHAPTER XXIV

I sympathized. Being in the orbit of a captivating, cultivated woman made me realize how much I yearned for the attentions of a friend and a lover, one who made my heart race and who was my equal in society and intellect. I had revelled in my affairs with Peggy Alexander and Jenny Clow, but I was ready for more. I yearned to be a companion and a protector where the happiness of my beloved was essential to my own.

Nancy McLehose's grace and vulnerability made her perfect for the lead female role in the Greek tragedy unfolding in my head. I sympathized with Burns because Clarinda was making us both miserable. But it was clear—to me at least—he was merely passing through her orbit. His intentions, known to me if not her, were far from honourable. And to be candid, I did not believe Burns, for all his native genius and polished manners, was high-born enough for her.

Quite how I deluded myself that I, the son of a laird's steward, was worthy, I cannot explain. But I saw myself as a rising man of the law and just the kind of dashing blade she needed to shield her from all the ills of life. That desire burned all the brighter because she didn't even heed me beyond my usefulness as a suitable chaperone. I wasn't such a blockhead that I didn't realize that. Yet when I received a note from Clarinda asking me to visit her at my next convenience, I scurried forth, aware that I was learning to live on less pride than was my worth.

I was shown in by a sullen Jenny Clow, clearly grieved that I was visiting Clarinda alone, and greeted warmly by the mistress of the house, brisk and bubbly as sparkling Champagne wine. She was wearing an ivory, hand-sewn, silk gown that looked as if it had just arrived from Paris, and her auburn hair hung loosely over her bare shoulders. She seemed insensible to the effect her appearance had on me.

"Mr. Bruce....can I call you John? I do wish us to become good and close friends. I'd like to seek your counsel on your confrère, Mr. Burns."

The words stung like sweat in my eyes, but I maintained a kind of fixed, unnatural grin as she continued.

"Few are fortunate to relish such refined enjoyment as I have with the poet. That enjoyment has not led beyond the limits of virtue, but my reflections on our time together has not been altogether unmixed with regret," she said, leaning forward in her chair, her eyes dropping to the floor in resignation.

She explained that she was concerned the liaisons with Burns would cause pain to a friend to whom she was bound by what she called the sacred ties of gratitude. I surmised she meant her cousin William Craig. Her second worry was that the poet might get the wrong impression owing to her unreservedness and be repulsed. With great effort, I strove to reassure her that Burns might find it in himself to look beyond any behaviour he found unbecoming or vulgar.

But above all, she was troubled that Heaven might not approve of the union, given her complicated situation. “I cannot serve two masters,” she said. As I gazed into those lovely eyes, I reassured her—as much for my sake as for the poet’s—that her reputation and religion were not at risk.

She seemed to be heartened by the conversation and was in no rush for our audience to come to an end. For my part, I imagined her as Penelope to my Odysseus, devoted and waiting faithfully for 25 years for me to return from the Trojan Wars. Even her trilling about the day’s weather sounded to my infatuated ears like Homer’s masterpiece.

CHAPTER XXV

Clark's Tavern at the head of Fleshmarket Close was like a busy ant colony. Bodies spilled out the door into the close, such was the throng of drinkers and revellers. Burns and I eased our way through the gangs of workers from the nearby butchery and other flotsam that had washed up in this notorious watering hole. Clark's was less a place of conviviality than of business—that is if your business was gaming, whoring or cockfighting.

Thankfully, Brodie was a slave to all of these passions, and we found him settled in around a table playing cards with three other men.

Burns played his part well, feigning surprise at finding the dandyish Deacon of the Guild in such a den of iniquity. "Master Brodie, I never took you for an aficionado of such timeless and ubiquitous vice," he said with a wink toward me.

Brodie's lip curled. "Sir, I never thought to see you in this fine establishment," he said. "Perhaps the Duchess of Gordon has found a new sideshow in Count Boruwlaski, the celebrated Polish dwarf who I hear is visiting town."

Burns laughed off the insult. "I hear Count Barrel of Whisky is an entertaining dinner companion, much more amusing than the dull fare I served up to polite society."

As the two duelled, the card game went on. Two of Brodie's comrades had English accents, and in one—an unpleasant-looking, sharp-featured fellow with cold eyes—I felt sure we had found our Humphrey Moore.

"What game is it you play?" inquired Burns.

"It is called Pope Joan," said Brodie. "Come join the table, my fellows, and I would happily lighten your purse."

Again, Burns made light. "I'm sure you would, but perhaps I'll watch a while to get its measure."

The cards were dealt, and Brodie turned to Burns. Despite his obvious dislike of the poet, he seemed determined to impress him. "The game is named after the legend that Pope John the Eighth was actually a woman, a story that naturally riles the Catholic Church but endears itself to staunch Presbyterians such as those arranged around this table."

The game played itself out, and when Brodie produced the nine of diamonds, the other players let out a groan of capitulation as the deacon gathered the money sitting on the table.

"The red nine – the so-called Curse of Scotland. Did you know that, Mr. Burns?" asked Brodie.

"I have heard it called such. I was told it was because The Butcher Cumberland wrote his orders on the back of such a card on the eve of Culloden," replied the poet.

"Not so. The nickname predates that messy affair by many years. It originates in this very card game. Since the Curse of Scotland must be something Scots hate and detest, what could be more fitting than the Pope? The nine of diamonds is Pope, the most powerful card in the game, and so it is also the Curse of Scotland."

"Well I am now better informed, if no wiser. Thank you, sir."

I left them talking while I gathered two whiskies, but when I returned, Burns was regaling Brodie with his future plans. "I had planned to close my late meteor-like appearance on this stage of life by returning to the toil of a country farmer, but I find I could only fight for existence in the same miserable manner that I saw a venerable parent succumb. As such, I have applied to become an officer of excise."

"Tax collectors are not as beloved as poets," noted Brodie.

"They are surely not. But the excise is awash with silver. Look at William Younger, the brewer. He was an exciseman, and his good fortune in tobacco seizures helped support his brewery.

"Why, just the other day I was in at the General Excise Office in Chessel's Court for an examination. There was talk that a cutter carrying large quantities of tea and brandy was captured just off Leith. All that contraband and all the money from taxes all over Scotland sit in that office with nary a pistol to protect it. My first act as a gauger would be to suggest it all be placed behind the portcullis of Edinburgh Castle for safekeeping.

"Anyway, gentlemen, my friend Mr. Bruce and I have to beg your forgiveness for distracting you from your game. We have to take our leave."

With that he stood up and eased his way out of the tavern. But he need not have worried about causing offence. The four players were staring at one another, their tongues lolling. The seed had been firmly planted.

CHAPTER XXVI

The next day I wandered down North Bridge toward Burns' attic at St. James Square. As I ascended the stairs, I passed the figure of Jenny Clow coming down, adjusting her bodice. I was so startled, I barely had time to inquire into her well-being and, more pertinently, what she was doing there.

She flushed when she saw me. "I was just delivering a letter for Mr. Burns from the mistress," she protested rather too vociferously before bustling on.

I stood there, gums flapping like a sea trout, but no sound came forth. I knew he was unscrupulous when it came to the fairer sex, but surely Burns wasn't being false to the woman to whom he'd just days before professed undying devotion?

When I stood before him, I knew he was. "Please tell me you are not enjoying the mercenary embraces of Clarinda's servant girl?" I raged.

"Why should I not? You are. And there is nothing mercenary about the transaction—she is a minx and enjoys the game."

"But what about Clarinda? You have just penned a poem calling her the mistress of your soul!"

He had not deviated so far from the road of common decency that he did not look slightly shamed at this. He tried to excuse himself by claiming Jenny offered sweet relief from the pressures crushing him from all sides—Creech had yet to pay him for the Edinburgh Edition; his brother Gilbert was in financial difficulties and requesting aid; Jean Armour had been turned out by her father when he discovered she was pregnant again. 'An unlucky affair' was how he characterized his latest brush with fatherhood.

But that was all self-serving hogwash. His talk of celebrating women like a 'starry sky on a frosty December night' was an evasion of truth, which was that he seduced them as he enjoyed their youth and vitality and then betrayed and abandoned them. Burns professed himself a lover of the fairer sex, but in that moment he seemed to me as parasitic as a lamprey eel.

I felt like scales had fallen from my eyes—as if he had betrayed me too. In fact, the fault was mine. I had idealized him, built him into a figure like the statue in King Nebuchadnezzar's dream. But like the statue, the poet had feet of clay.

"You must resolve to end matters with Clarinda," I thundered. "Because if you don't, I swear to God I will tell her of this."

Now, it was the poet's turn to raise his hackles. He squared up to me and placed his face inches from my nose.

"Spare me your fastidious pomp, you young whelp. You have no sense but that life is a fairy scene. With ripening age, in comes the gravity of hoary wisdom, and all the dear bewitching phantoms are wickedly chased away," he roared. The outburst drained him, and he retreated to his chair, rubbing his brow.

I was close to tears but had nothing left to say. My chest and my stomach were raw and sore. It felt like someone had stepped on my heart. I turned and walked out, determined that I was done with him.

CHAPTER XXVII

But I could not do it. To break with Sylvander would have meant breaking with Clarinda, too. I visited Potterrow the next day on Nancy's invitation, avoiding eye contact with Jenny Clow, and she with me.

Nancy was quick to reassure me that the line of decorum may have been infringed but it had not been crossed. "May those benevolent spirits, whose office it is to save the fall of virtue struggling on the brink of vice, be ever present to protect and guide us in right paths," she said piously.

She had confided with her minister, the Reverend John Kemp, and he had counselled that in her current state of married bondage, her relationship with Burns should remain a friendship. I tried to not sound too vigorous in my endorsement of the good reverend, but she appeared to be resolved. "I wish our feelings were more moderate, but why set one's heart on impossibilities?" she asked rhetorically.

Yet beneath her resignation and his betrayal was a genuine passion. Each saw in the other a solution to their respective predicaments, a path to a better future. When they were together, they could forget about the world for a while.

But they could not ignore the world's disapprobation of their union. Kemp had not only counselled Nancy, he had written a letter of admonition that she gave me and asked me to share with the poet. She wrote a brief covering letter which said, among other things, that the "storms of life will pass…I trust we'll meet in a place where love is not a crime. I charge you to meet me there. Oh God, I must lay down my pen."

As she handed me the packet, she was in tears. I longed to hold her and tell her I'd be the friend, companion and protector she had long sought. But her tears were spilling for Burns, mourning a relationship that she knew could never be. I felt crushed but strangely blessed to have been in the presence of such tenderness. I touched my lips to her hand and departed before my heart left me undone.

I was debating how to approach Burns, following our quarrel the previous day, when I came upon Peter Hill, Creech's clerk, who told me the poet was in Johnnie Dowie's tavern and was in hearty mood.

I found him slumped over a bowl. I sat down next to him and waited for him to speak first. He took a long draft and turned to me. "I have drunk her health twice tonight. She is all that my soul holds dear in this world. I love her to madness," he said quietly.

"I know. She has had that effect on many a poor fool," I replied. "I have a letter from her. You will not like it, so you had best brace yourself."

He read the covering letter and then the note of admonition from Kemp. His face remained stony, but his neck reddened and his jugular vein began to pulse wildly. He crumpled the letter and threw it in the fire.

"This is a passion inspired by the purest flame, but the half-inch soul of an unfeeling, cold-blooded, pitiful Presbyterian bigot cannot forgive it. I despise his jealousy and his spying," he raged.

Once the storm had passed, he slumped again. "My God, I have to get out of Edinburgh and head for Dumfries. But I must see her one last time. John, I know I have tested your patience, but I beg that you aid me in gaining an audience with the star of all my hopes before I leave for the West."

We were living in the age of enlightenment. Natural philosophers had calculated the movement of the stars. But none could chart the madness of men afflicted by the exquisite bliss of love.

CHAPTER XXVIII

I do not doubt that Burns loved Nancy in the moment. But he could be a cynical dreamer—one minute ardent and enraptured, the next restrained and hard-hearted. After a day or two of mulling over his predicament, he sounded as if he had made a full recovery from his recent anguish.

I had kept my distance since our falling out but still moved within the poet's orbit, including a convening of the Crochallan Fencibles in Dawnie Douglas' tavern. I was close enough to hear him tell the shambling figure of William Smellie that he had recently scraped within a hair's breadth of the breach of love.

"Thank my stars I got off heart-whole," he said, slapping Smellie on the back. I stared at him across the table, banged down my cup on the table and departed the tavern to quizzical stares from the members of Edinburgh's foremost drinking militia.

The only explanation I could fathom for such a sea change in his mood was that the breach he talked about was in the fortifications protecting Clarinda's virtue. I contrived an excuse to visit Potterrow, ostensibly with news about Burns' imminent departure—he was heading to Ayrshire to see what aid he could offer his brother and Jean Armour.

The door was answered by the lady of the house herself—looking more tousled than the carefully coiffured figure I'd known to this point. But it only made her more glorious in my eyes.

She said she was in such distress, she'd sent Jenny Clow away. She gave no indication she knew that her servant had been serving both the mistress of the house and her lover. But it seemed clear to me that is exactly what Burns had become. Nancy all but admitted that his persistence had finally worn down her defenses.

"I do not blame anyone but myself, but I cannot see him again until I can depend on myself to act otherwise," she said. "My eternal happiness depends on adherence to virtue, and I feel I cannot serve two masters. God pity me." She took my hand in hers and gave me her flirtatious smile.

Unfortunately for my own pursuit of happiness, the news that the poet was leaving town made her more, not less, devoted to him—he could remain a friend, able, in her words, to 'caress the mental intelligence as he would the corporeal frame' but would no longer be a threat to her good character. I plodded back to Mrs. Carfrae's cold abode in a state of considerable misery at the unfairness of it all.

My mood was scarcely improved some days later when a packet landed from Burns, who had arrived in Mauchline in his native Ayrshire. He implored me to continue as his emissary to Clarinda. He was a man who could often see into people's souls, yet he was oblivious to my love for the woman whose affections he was toying with so rashly. Or perhaps he wasn't oblivious but knew that my Don Quixote-like knight errant's adventure was doomed.

Either way, he taxed my loyalty to the limit. He wrote

to Clarinda that he had met with the heavily pregnant Jean but could not endure her. "I am disgusted with her," said the letter. "I tried to compare her with my Clarinda, but it was setting the expiring glimmer of a farthing taper besides the cloudless glory of the meridian sun. I have done with her, and she with me." I watched as Nancy clucked over the news with satisfaction and even passed to me a small shirt she had made for Burns' son.

Yet less than two weeks later he wrote to me to say that he had moved the heavily pregnant Jean in with a local doctor, John Mackenzie, who was an old friend of his. "I found Jean with her cargo very well laid in but unfortunately moored at the mercy of wind and tide," he said. "I have towed her into a convenient harbour, where she may lie snug until she unloads, and have taken the command myself."

Burns' duplicity scattered the residue of respect and esteem in which I held him. His account was explicit and shabby:

"I have fucked her till she rejoiced with joy unspeakable and full of glory. I swore her privately and solemnly never to attempt any claim on me as a husband. She did all this like a good girl, and I took the opportunity of some dry horse litter and gave her such a thundering bombardment that electrified the very marrow of her bones. Oh what a peacemaker is a well-placed pintle—the mediator, the guarantor, the umpire, the bond of union."

I knew of his capacity for coarseness but never for callousness. He truly believed that poets operated according to different rules of propriety than the 'sober sons of judgment and prudence'.

But true poets radiated hot passion, not cold contempt.

CHAPTER XXIX

Consumed as I was by the web of deceit enveloping Burns, sensational events elsewhere reduced the affairs of the poet to an afterthought in the gossip running up and down the Royal Mile.

Edinburgh's winter had dragged into March, and there was snow on the ground as I trudged down Carrubber's Close to the offices of Samuel Mitchelson, WS. The bells of St. Giles had hardly rung eight, and I was still shaking the snow from my hat and coat when I noticed a brooding presence sitting in a chair next to old Mr. Beattie The aged accountant was in his customary pose, hunched over a ledger and turning the colour of a plum with his mental exertions. The large man beside him was a studied contrast, as effortlessly regal as if he wore a crown. Archibald Cockburn, the sheriff-depute, was not in the habit of making house calls, and he appeared unimpressed at having had to wait.

"Is it prejudice against the law or against your clients that you choose to work just half the day?" chided Cockburn. I muttered a nervous apology and ushered his lumbering frame into the office I shared with David Balfour, who thankfully was out of town. He would have demanded to know the reason Midlothian's most senior judge had come to call on its most lowly legal apprentice. Old Mr. Beattie seemed scarcely to have noticed even a presence as looming as Cockburn.

He removed his coat and proceeded straight to business. "Master Bruce, when you and your...client came to see me, you mentioned you had some suspicions about the plague of robberies in our fair city but not enough evidence to 'justify tearing a man from the bosom of society,' to use your words. I'd like you to share those suspicions with me," he said, staring down a bulbous nose on which his glasses were balanced precariously.

"May I inquire if there has been any progress in the case, your Lordship?" I ventured.

He continued staring down his nose, unblinking, as if there were a rank smell in the room. But then he relented. "Given your considerable assistance, I think it fair to share with you that the offer of pardon was enticing enough to lure one of the despicable wretches involved into giving up his fellow degenerates. They attempted to rob the Excise Office in Chessel's Court but were disturbed before they could steal anything more than petty cash," explained Cockburn.

I rejoiced silently at the news Burns' plan had worked. But I was puzzled. "If you have them, why do you want to hear my half-baked hypothesis, sir?" I asked.

"The case is not yet cracked," he said. "The man who calls himself John Brown said he had but £4 in his pocket from the raid on the Excise Office, which he said yielded £16. He gave up two rogues called Andrew Ainslie and George Smith, the grocer on the Cowgait. Yet there were clearly four in the gang or the arithmetic on the division of the illicit spoils does not work. Brown, for now, is silent on the matter, holding out to guarantee his pardon. Who do you think that fourth man might be, Master Bruce?" With that, Cockburn reclined back, showing me that he had revealed fully as much as he intended to.

I had no choice but to play my full hand, relishing the sight of a senior judge who thought he'd heard everything stare at me slack-jawed when I mentioned Brodie's name. I told him Peggy Alexander had learned about Brown's real identity from the whore Annie Johnson, that her caddie friend had placed Brown as an associate of Ainslie, Smith and Brodie in the den of iniquity known as Clark's Tavern, and that Burns had planted the idea of a raid on the Excise Office in the minds of the felonious quartet.

Cockburn recovered his composure, nodded slowly, then reclaimed his coat and hat. "You have been a great help, Master Bruce. The science of criminal investigation is a guessing game unless of course you know all the facts in advance," he said, and a half smile cracked his imperious features. "Tell your lady friend that her silks will be recovered and returned. I believe they may have been taken to Chesterfield, in Derbyshire, to be sold by a villainous innkeeper of Brown's acquaintance. But we will find them."

As soon as he'd gone, I grabbed my coat and went looking for Jamie, the young Highland caddie who had befriended Peggy Alexander. She'd been forced to move from Baxter's Close after Lord Moray's financial collapse, and I had not seen her since her departure. I was intoxicated with the news Cockburn had brought, and I was bursting to tell Peggy that her deliverance was at hand.

I found Jamie at the Luckenbooths and asked if he knew where to find her. His response was worrying.

"Aye, I know where to find her, but you might regret the quest," he said with a shake of the head.

"How so?" I queried.

"She has lost regard for decency and decorum. She would now as willingly lay with a chimney sweep as she used to with a lord," he said flatly.

I asked him to show me, nonetheless. We made our way down the snow-covered, crowded High Street and crossed the filthy gutters to go down Fleshmarket Close to Clark's Tavern. The squalor and dissolution seemed more apparent somehow amid the light dusting of snow.

"She'll be in there," said Jamie, gesturing with his thumb before walking away disconsolately.

It was early, but Clark's was doing roaring trade, as workers from the nearby slaughterhouse finished their night shift, having supplied the stalls on the High Street with their fresh supply of flesh. There was a fetid smell of blood and stale beer mixed with that of the cheap scented water favoured by the ladies of pleasure who frequented the place.

I found Peggy wrapped in the arms of a sailor. I tapped her shoulder and said, "Peggy, I need to talk to you. I have good news about your silks."

She turned, focused in foggy fashion and then abandoned her sailor in order to embrace me. She was a queer, wild sight. The sailor took exception to this transfer of affections and wrestled her away before facing up to me. "Where are your manners, boy?" he demanded. "I have worked like a galley slave to earn silver to pay for this wench. Find your own doxy."

I talked past him. "The plan worked," I shouted. "You will get your silks back. Come with me now."

Peggy smiled in groggy fashion, as if drunk. "What need have I for silk? The Church of Scotland's General Assembly meets soon—it's the busiest time of the year," she giggled.

But her face dropped as she leaned in to whisper in my ear. "I have a pox, John," she said. "They gave me poison to cure me, but it has made me mad."

She must have meant mercury, a common treatment for social diseases but one that if maladministered was known to melt the brain.

"Goodbye, John Bruce. You made me happy, if ever so briefly. I will see you down the road, my jo," she said.

She kissed me tenderly on the cheek, and I felt a tear. But then she whirled around and pulled her sailor back to the table where the noisy revelry resumed. I turned and left, her tears mixing freely with my own. I never did see her again, but I heard from Jamie that she died soon after.

It was the last of my involvement in the infamous Deacon Brodie affair, but the case was riveting for everyone in Auld Reekie. Ainslie and Smith were taken to the Tolbooth, but Brodie caught wind of his imminent arrest and fled to London by stagecoach, just ahead of a warrant, a £150-reward notice and a King's Messenger sent to track him down. He was traced to a hotel in Amsterdam and found hiding in a cupboard the day before he planned to sail for America. Since robbing the Excise Office was a capital offence, his guilt was a foregone conclusion. It was an irony worthy of his incredible story that he was hanged at the west end of the Luckenbooths, before 40,000 of his countrymen, on the very same gibbet he had worked to improve. He was the first to test the fruits of his labour.

I take no pride in recounting that I was as eager as the next man to see the macabre spectacle of Brodie taking the last drop. As big a crowd as ever to assemble in Edinburgh gathered on a sunny afternoon in early October. I could barely see the scaffold, able to make out just the heads of the captain of the City Guard and the masked hangman as well as the two nooses dangling from a great oak beam.

But my vantage point was close to the 50 guards who marched the two unchained prisoners, Brodie and George Smith, the short distance from the cells for the Tolbooth's condemned to the execution spot. The crowd roared when they saw the procession.

The deacon, hair dressed and powdered, looked every inch the Edinburgh gentleman, wearing what looked like a fresh black suit, embroidered waistcoat, white stockings and black buckled shoes. He was, it appeared, resolved to leave this world with a dignity he had rarely shown while living in it.

I moved closer to the scaffold where I could see the magistrates in their ceremonial robes standing in attendance. After Brodie had climbed the scaffold steps, he nodded to the magistrates and then turned to the crowd and gave a deep bow. The mob, many of whom were sympathetic to Brodie's attempt to rob the government, cheered loudly. He drew a handkerchief from his pocket, laid it on the platform and knelt to pray as a silence descended on the crowd. He rose, thanked the attending reverend and shook Smith's hand.

The two men were handed white nightcaps to put over their heads and white handkerchiefs to drop as a signal they were ready. The giant bell of St. Giles tolled at intervals, as a solemn hush descended on the crowd.

Brodie lightened the mood by ascending the steps at speed, before pulling on the noose to test it, which generated another cheer.

He pulled the nightcap over his head and dropped his handkerchief, and the trap gave way. The crowd roared as his feet tried in vain to find purchase, finally dancing wildly in thin air. And that was the end of Deacon William Brodie.

As we walked away, I heard a man say, "It was a good end to an ill life. It is to be hoped he makes better of it in the next world."

CHAPTER XXX

Deacon Brodie's inglorious exit was still some months hence when word had arrived from Ayrshire that Jean Armour had given birth to twins—and that both had died. I remained the faithful lapdog to both the star-crossed lovers. Burns wrote saying he had resolved on farming Patrick Miller's stony outcrop near Dumfries but would take his excise instruction lest the land's fecundity was limited to rabbits and rocks.

"I have two plans in life before me, and I wish to adopt the one most likely to procure me independence," he said. His letter was full of anxious forebodings, as his future existence was buffeted by winds he could not control. Creech, the publisher, had not paid him for his second edition; he had just lost two children; he bore responsibilities toward Jean; he feared he had just made a 'poet's choice, not a farmer's choice' in taking up the plough at the estate called Ellisland; and to cap it all Clarinda was in an accusatory mood.

"He writes me but once a week, and his silence causes me pain," she said, unburdening herself to me on a visit to Potterrow. "He is so fickle—one day, the life of a farmer, the next it is the excise. A thousand conjectures have made me most unhappy."

I was scarcely less frustrated with the poet and his cold inconsistencies. I told him so in a letter that declined the continued role of emotional intermediary.

Yet, as so often when Burns had roved beyond the paling fence of common decency, he spun his words into a tender spell that had the most sympathetic effect on his reader.

"Had I the least glimmering hope that Clarinda's charms could ever have been mine, things would have been different," he wrote to me. "Life is no great blessing, and at least the dark means an end to pain, care, woes and wants. But a man, conscious of having acted an honest part among his fellow creatures, even granting that he may have been the sport, at times, of passions and instincts, goes to the great unknown Being with nothing to fear since He gave him those passions and instincts and well knows their force."

Yet he was still not forthright about his intentions to Clarinda, even if they were apparent to anyone whose eyes were not blinded by the scales of adoration. Burns returned to Edinburgh, just as the Brodie affair was at fever pitch, to settle with Creech, sign the lease for Ellisland with Patrick Miller but mainly, he said, to resolve his affair of the heart.

He visited her several times that week, careless to what Clarinda's neighbours or benefactor might say, and so in no need of a chaperone.

I arranged to meet him on his way back from visiting Clarinda and we wandered down the Lawnmarket, turned on Libberton's Wynd and walked beneath the painted sign into Johnnie Dowie's tavern as we had done so many times.

"Come away in, gentlemen, there's corn in Egypt yet," proclaimed the rosy-nosed landlord with same ready chorus that always greeted us.

But Burns was not the same peasant dandy I'd first met just 18 months earlier. Dissipation had been replaced by resolution, mirth with stoicism.

He had arrived in Edinburgh with a sense of possibility but no firm idea of what he hoped to achieve. Having learned from hard experience that the great world would never accept the independence of thought and action he coveted, he was now resolved to abandon polite society and retire to the countryside. "I have undergone a revolution in my mind and now have a serious aim. Though poor by comparison to the last 18 months, it is luxury in comparison to my preceding life," he said as we stood waiting for our wine.

We found our way to The Coffin where Willie Nicol sat fulminating over a bowl. "Don't mention to Willie anything of the Clarinda affair. He would be hurt if he knew I had not confided in him," whispered the poet.

The short-tempered schoolmaster scowled at our arrival. He sat in roughly the same spot as I had first encountered him, and he appeared to be wearing the same garb—a bottle green jacket haphazardly pulled over a green waistcoat, which had the effect of enhancing his mottled, dishevelled appearance.

"Here he is, Christ-less Bobbie and the Devil's apprentice," said Nicol. Apparently the two had been having an argument about Burns' views on religion and monarchy, both of which went against the prevailing wind.

Nicol shared both Burns' nonconformist views and antipathy toward the House of Hanover. But he argued discretion required the poet moderate his behaviour in public.

"There are reports of your imprudence, namely refusing to stand in a theatre when the fiddlers played God Save the King. Have you been inflicted with idiocy?" asked Nicol. The poet did not take offence, well used to the schoolmaster's blunt manners.

"So what should I have done? Betrayed every principle I hold dear?" replied Burns.

"You should have behaved like the famous Vicar of Bray who was a Papist, then a Protestant, then a Papist, then a Protestant again under the Tudors. When he was accused of being a turncoat, he replied, 'Not so, for I have always kept to my principle, which is this—to live and die the Vicar of Bray,'" said Nicol with uncharacteristic humour.

Burns bowed deeply and sallied back: "O thou are wisest of the wise. How infinitely indebted is your rattle-headed slave that from thy luminous path of right-lined rectitude thou can lookest benignly down on an unerring wretch."

Nicol feigned touchiness. "Ach! The Devil has flown off with you. Beware, young Bruce, or he will have his talons in you, too. To business, I have an old bay mare that I can loan you for your farming venture. I called her Peg Nicholson, after that mad woman who tried to murder our even madder king. The latest rumour is that George tried to shake hands with a tree, thinking it to be the King of Prussia. What a line of blockheads."

Burns laughed and shook his head. "I am touched by your generosity, but I fear you may also be touched if this is how you would have me endear myself to the friends of Hanover. That said, I will borrow your mare and try her with the plough."

Nicol, who had clearly been in residence for some considerable time, excused himself. "Keep up the witty wickedness, gentlemen. I must retire to consider new measures of indiscriminate harshness with which to drive my idiot charges," he said as he made his way to the door.

Once he was gone, I grilled Burns. "How goes it with Clarinda?" I asked, hoping I did not sound unnaturally inquisitive. It was only days after he had buried his still-born children, but he appeared to have recovered from his grief.

The poet shook his head and sighed. "Life is a weary, barren path and woe be to him who ventures on it alone. Clarinda is the dearest partner of my soul, and we will make our pilgrimage together. I will always let her know how I go on and with what adventures I meet. I will love her to death, through death and forever," he said without self-pity.

"But.....?" I prompted him.

"But I have to make some sacrifices. You have not met my beguiling young Ayrshire hussy, but I am inclined to give her matrimonial title. She has not been part of my inner life in the way that I have shared my soul with Clarinda. But she will make an agreeable companion for the rest of my journey through life."

I wasn't disposed to dissuade him from the match, but it struck me as queer that he was so quick to plight his troth to someone with whom he shared so little in the realm of the spirit. I raised the question, and he waved away the concern.

"If I have not got polite tattle, modish manners and fashionable dress, I do have the comeliest figure and the kindest heart in the country," he said.

"Have you told Clarinda?"

"I presented her with a pair of drinking glasses this evening, and the mood would have been ruined by broaching the subject," he said. "To be frank, I don't know how to tell her. But it must be done if I am to have the stability of mind I require."

My own selfish interest in Clarinda required that the poet exit the stage, so I meekly nodded my concurrence. He took that as my blessing for his new course and thumped me on the back and laughed. "You are a worthy young fellow, John Bruce. Worthy indeed," he said.

He took off for the West the next day to be instructed in the art of gauging for the excise, a last resort if the fortunes of the farming project failed him.

But it was no surprise when I received news in late May that he had married Jean and was intent on moving her to Ellisland with him. He seemed resigned to, if not rejoicing at, the prospect of his new existence.

"I am so enamoured," he wrote, "with a certain girl's prolific twin-bearing merit that I have given her legal title to the best blood in my body. To be serious my worthy friend, I found I had a long and much-loved fellow creature's happiness and misery in my hands.

"I foresaw this from the beginning. Ambition could not form a higher wish than to be wedded to novelty. But I have retired to my shades with a little comfortable pride and a few comfortable pounds. Tomorrow I begin my operations as farmer. God speed the plough."

CHAPTER XXXI

The curious thing was that Burns' muse, which had been silent for much of the time he spent in the gilded cage of Edinburgh, burst into song after he moved to rural Nithsdale. In the capital, his output shrivelled in ambition and humanity. True, he mended some old songs for James Johnson's Scots Musical Museum. But anyone who judged the poet by his woeful Address to Edinburgh—"Edina! Scotia's darling seat..."—might have wondered what all the fuss was about. He'd attempted to ingratiate himself with his patrons in the capital, and the effort did him an injustice. Yet back in his rural roots, he rediscovered his voice.

"I muse and rhyme morning, noon and night and have a hundred different poetic plans floating in the region of fancy, somewhere between purpose and resolve," he wrote me.

The farm had its own anxieties, no doubt, but he was at least free from the pressures of the literary world. He sent me some verses that suggested he was sanguine about his choices, such as:

"Happiness is but a name,
Make content and ease thy aim.
Ambition is a meteor gleam;
Fame a restless, airy dream."

They were words befitting a man who had blazed a trail across Edinburgh's skyline like a comet.

But he also sent on some more pastoral poetic schemes, one of which was dedicated to a former lover, Mary Campbell, who he told me died before she and Burns could emigrate to Jamaica:

> *"Flow gently, sweet Afton! amang thy green braes,*
> *Flow gently, I'll sing thee a song in thy praise;*
> *My Mary's asleep by thy murmuring stream,*
> *Flow gently, sweet Afton, disturb not her dream."*

The pity was that I did not send such a soothing rhyme to Nancy McLehose before she found out about the poet's furtive assignments with Jenny Clow.

I had seen little of the former Clarinda through the summer and autumn of that year—my usefulness to her had clearly run its course and I was resigned in misery to her being as unattainable as the Honours of Scotland, the Crown jewels kept under lock and key in Edinburgh Castle.

She had sent one letter to me but it was entirely devoted to inquiries about the poet. Since I did not relish being the bearer of bad news, I had not replied, assuming—wrongly as it turned out—that Burns would eventually make good on his promise to tell her himself.

But just as the days reached their shortest, Nancy appeared at the offices of Samuel Mitchelson, WS, in Carrubber's Close, causing something of a scandal. Even old Mr. Beattie lifted his head from his rows and columns to note the presence of an unchaperoned young lady. Yet such was her agitation, she was oblivious to this breach of convention. She looked breathtaking, sporting a rustic look that suited her face and figure—a simple, low-cut bodice with pleated neckline, silk brocade shoes with buckles and a jaunty, broad-brimmed "shepherdess" hat in the modern style. The thought crossed my mind that it may have been Burns' influence that persuaded her to abandon the more formal, courtly style favoured by high society.

I secured a quiet corner of the office and asked after her welfare.

The inquiry provoked a diamond of water and salt to trickle down her pretty face.

"I have been betrayed, John, as I'm sure you are aware," she said, raising her pretty nose in an act of defiance.

"I'm not sure to what you refer," I stammered, trying to ascertain more precisely which betrayal she had unearthed.

"Word reached me from Dumfries that Mr. Burns has married the mother of his poor dead children," she said. "I grieve that he and I could never be together in this life, but that is the price of love. I can sympathize with his desire for stability and independence. As such, even though he was less than frank with me, when I found out about his bond with Jean Armour, I wished all good things attend him.

"However, what I cannot tolerate is the treachery with my own servant girl. Jenny Clow gave birth to the poet's child this past week. The poor wretch is untended and was forced to turn to me for charity. And yet that villain lays claim to the title of honest man. He should be exposed on the pillory of derision." She spat the last words with a vitriol I would never have suspected she possessed.

She said she had urged Jenny to issue a writ seeking financial support from the poet and asked me to communicate the news to him. Every atom of my being urged me to tell her how I felt about her, but it was apparent even to me that my love for her was as forlorn and pathetic as was her obsession with Burns. It simply wasn't meant to be.

As soon as she left, I wrote to the poet with the news and received a terse response saying that he would journey to the capital to settle the affair early in the new year. "I must again trouble you to find and secure me a direction where to find Jenny Clow, for the main part of my business in Edinburgh is to settle the matter with her and free her hand of the process," he wrote without any of his usual frippery.

I secured Jenny's lodging place from Nancy and I gather Burns took ownership of his son, even offering to take the boy into his home, but the mother would not part with him. It was only when word reached the poet that Jenny was dying of tuberculosis that he ventured north to the capital in the early winter of 1791.

We met on a raw day in the tavern at White Hart Inn, where he had taken a room, in the Grassmarket. The poet looked leaner and windswept, as befit a man out in all weathers, smartly clad in corduroy breeches, dark blue stockings, a long-tailed coat and a broad blue bonnet. I shook his hand warmly but with some trepidation. We had communicated infrequently in the past year, and I was not at all sure about his mood. It turned out it could be summed up in a word—volatile.

He was pleased to see me, back in the crucible of so much past revelry.

"I'm anxious about your spiritual welfare and growth in grace, so I urge that you hear me on this—the Plenipotentiary, a bawdy work of a Captain Morris who should be conferred as an immediate familiar of the Crochallan Fencibles," he said.

He cleared his throat theatrically and recited the verse about the great-pintled Turk from the Barbary shore who became an immediate sensation at the Court of St. James and at the theatre. He concluded:

> *"The nymphs of the stage did his ramrod engage,*
> *Made him free of their gay seminary;*
> *And Italian signoras opened all their back doors*
> *To the great Plenipotentiary."*

We laughed together, as we did so often in more carefree days. But he was clearly plagued by low spirits.

"Does the farm flourish?" I asked.

"Man, I'm at the elbow of existence. It has been a ruinous affair," he replied darkly, taking a long draft of his claret. "That farm will be a very, very hard bargain, if practicable at all. I have 10 cows and four servants who are little removed from the brutes they drive. So much for farming." He shook his head in exasperation.

"My brother Gilbert's lease is near expiring, and he may be able to live by my assistance. I will throw myself into the excise where I am sure of immediate and constant bread," he said. He explained he'd met the head collector in Dumfries, and between them they had engineered a vacancy by removing the incumbent tax collector—an opening that Burns intended to fill.

"I know how the word 'exciseman,' or still more opprobrious 'gauger,' will sound to your ears. I too have seen the day when my auditory nerves would have felt very delicately on this subject. But a wife and children are things which have a wonderful power in blunting these kinds of sensations," he lamented. Jean was pregnant again, and the prospect had concentrated the poet's mind.

"Does the government know it is employing its enemy?" I joked.

"Along with revelry and seduction, I have forsaken the dark stroke of politics," he replied. "Treasonous and seditious works could never flow from the quill of the faithful, loyal subject I have become."

I diverted him with all the news from the capital. He was most interested in the fate of a young English woman called Margaret Matthews who had come to his attention when she adopted the name Burns and set up a whore house on Rose Street near his former lodgings. The neighbours had complained and the city council had moved to banish the madam Burns from its borders.

The poet expressed much hilarity at the development. "You can be certain that the flinty-bosomed judges and lords prosecuting the case most vigorously were also lusty in taking advantage of such female frailty," he laughed. "I suggest we get exceedingly drunk and toast the fair Clarinda."

He winked at me. My clandestine love for her was obviously less concealed than I had hoped.

CHAPTER XXXII

I had arranged for us to visit Potterrow the next day. Nancy knew where Jenny Clow and her son were lodging and had agreed to take us there.

The morning was as frosty as the reception we received when we were shown into the apartment.

Nancy looked as beautiful as a rose, but it was as if the thorns had pierced her heart.

She stood as tall as her diminutive frame could manage and through taut lips inquired about Mrs. Burns.

"One of our mutual friends passed on to me that she is a kind body, if somewhat round and fat," she said. "But they were critical of your house as ill-contrived and dirty. Our friend said you mix in society in Dumfries, but no attention is paid by any person of rank to your wife."

"It is good to see you too, madam," said Burns. "My pile of rocks may well be ill-contrived but my marriage was not. My Jean is a plump bonny bird because she's four months gone."

The news stung Nancy and set her on her heels. Burns pressed home his advantage. "You tell the world that I am a villain and should be exposed on the pillory of derision," he said.

Nancy beamed poison toward me—I had passed on her words to the poet verbatim.

"But while I dare to sin, I dare not lie. Jenny Clow had the misfortune to make me a father, and it is with contrition that I own it," said Burns, and he bowed his head.

Nancy composed herself and her own posture softened. "That's as well. Jenny has been obliged to quit her service and is gone to a room without common necessaries where she is, to all appearances, dying. In circumstances so distressing, to whom can she so naturally look for aid as to the father of her child, a man for whose sake she has suffered many a sad and anxious night, shut from the world with no companions other than guilt and solitude? You now have an opportunity to evince that you indeed possess the fine feelings and humanity you have so often proclaimed."

I blended into the furniture as he stepped toward her and took her hand.

"For the sake of esteem and old friendship, how can I refuse? This tale of the poor girl's distress makes my heart weep blood. I would have taken my boy from her long ago had she had agreed to consent. But let us see what can be done for her relief," he gazed into her eyes with that hypnotic stare. "I still keep your silhouette in the sanctum sanctorum of my most anxious care. You are still the first of women, my ever beloved, my ever-sacred Clarinda."

He backed away a step and reached into his jacket pocket to withdraw a bundle of papers. "I have written some verses that I propose to dedicate to you and have set to some beautiful air. It begins, 'Ae fond kiss, and then we sever...'"

Nancy gently took the paper and read it slowly. A solitary tear rolled down her cheek as she recited the words:

> *"Had we never lov'd sae kindly*
> *Had we never lov'd sae blindly*
> *Never met—or never parted*
> *We'd have ne'er been broken-hearted."*

She broke down, weeping uncontrollably, and he took her in his arms and kissed her forehead, his own eyes misting as he considered perhaps that even he had not known the depth of his feelings until the hour of separation arrived.

He was crying. They were both crying. They kissed. Clarinda and Sylvander had taken centre stage once again, and I took their entrance as my cue to exit.

As I left, I heard Nancy comfort the poet who was by now in some distress. "Life is a short, passing scene," she said. "Trust that we will meet in happy eternity, in perfect and never-ending bliss."

EPILOGUE

It was a perfect late June evening, more than three years after the poet and Nancy had ended their love affair, as I walked down the High Street of the Royal Burgh of Dumfries. Gulls were cavorting across a cloudless sky as I walked past the town's medieval Midsteeple and into the Globe Inn.

Burns sat in his favourite haunt, like a shadow, unnoticed by his fellow drinkers. He was still handsome and dignified; when he lifted his head, the eyes remained clear, strong and probing. But he did not look like the same man who had set Edinburgh alight with his performance as the ploughman poet.

The intervening years had seen him hunched over a plough or huddled against the elements as he rode across the countryside collecting taxes for His Majesty's Excise. Perhaps it was his exertions that gave him a bowed appearance. But as he sat gazing contemplatively into the unlit fireplace, he exuded the air of resignation from a man beaten down by life.

When he saw me, the shade was replaced by sunshine. "John Bruce—there he stands strong as Samson and wise as Solomon. Come join me for a jug of claret," he said, fixing me with those piercing eyes that could see into people's souls.

He led me to his table and raised a glass. "May the companions of our youth be the friends of our old age," he proposed.

"So, have you steered so far to the north of the good opinion of the people of Dumfries that they won't take a drink with you?" I asked.

"Fame doesn't blow her trumpet for me as it used to, it's true. But more likely my townsmen are not over-fond of my politics. I have tried to be discreet about my sympathy for the land of liberty and equality, but it has brought me to the brink of destruction on more than one occasion. It was a rattle-headed, drunken boast, but most recently I offered a toast that our success in the war against revolutionary France should be equal to the justice of our cause."

"I can see how that might not have sat well with the Excise Board," I granted.

"They launched an inquiry into my political conduct on suspicion I was disaffected with the government," he said sheepishly.

"I also heard you dispatched a couple of guns to the French Convention?"

"That was a tale. We were after a smuggling schooner out in the Solway Firth. I was leading a division of dragoons, and we waded in breast high. They were firing at us from the vessel but couldn't get their great guns to bear on us. Once we got within 100 yards, the crew gave up the cause and took off over the side toward England. It was the Rosamond out of Plymouth. When they sold off her furniture, I bought four four-pounder carronade guns with carriages and grapeshot and had them shipped to France. That was before that perjured blockhead Louis went to the guillotine and they declared war on Britain, mind."

"You will go to your grave marching to your own drum," I said, shaking my head at the man's audacity, bearing in mind the source of his employment.

"And how goes it otherwise?"

"It goes, John. I'm 36 and I feel old already. Some days I'm so poorly I can scarcely hold up my pen and so deplorably stupid as not to be able to hold it to any purpose. The worst of it is, it's a disease of the spirit more than the body. The damn war has hit trade and means I am suffering a share of the pecuniary losses I can ill-bear. These irritations and some domestic vexations have left me at a low ebb. But listen to me! Social ostracism has made me lugubrious. How are your body and soul putting up? A little like man and wife, I suppose?"

"I'm well. Edinburgh and the law have been good to me, and since I was visiting a client in Moffat, I thought I'd come down to Dumfries and raise a bumper to a long-loved, dear friend."

"Blasted be the sacrilegious hand that attempts to sever that union," he said, hoisting his glass once again.

"I also have some news. Maybe you're not in the best mind to hear this, but I thought you'd want to know. I met Clarinda."

At the mention of her name, the poet stiffened and put down his glass.

"Clarinda.....recollection ruins me.....," his voice trailed off. He was silent for a time, and I could see his jaw clenching as he struggled to contain surfacing memories and emotions.

I broke the awkward silence. "She asked after you and your family. I wrote to you last year to say she had returned from Jamaica. She'd gone to rekindle relations with her fickle husband. What I didn't say was that it turned out he had a family by a coloured mistress, a fact she only discovered on landing in Kingston when no one was there to meet her from the ship. She made the return journey after three months but was plagued with ill-health and nervous disorders. She now seems much recovered and says she would welcome a letter from you—or even from Sylvander."

"Ah that's a role I haven't played for many years." Burns gazed into the fireplace and whispered:

"I'll ne'er blame my partial fancy,
Naething could resist my Nancy."

We took leave of the Globe and its boisterous, crimson-faced tipplers and wandered out into a fine summer's evening. Groups of well-dressed gentlemen and ladies were heading for a county ball but none deigned to recognize the poet.

"You have no plans to go to the ball, Rab?"

"No, no, my friend. That's all over now," he replied with a wave of his hand.

We walked in silence down toward the River Nith that runs broad and flat to the west of the town. As we watched some stevedores unloading coal and potatoes from a docked ship, Burns was clearly rapt in his own memories.

"This river has been the midwife to many of my creations. Often you don't know whether you're begetting a wise man or a fool," he laughed but was forced to stop in order to accommodate a hacking cough. "Damn, I should be quite in song at this time of year, yet the ravages of a life spent outdoors in foul weather plague me."

We walked away from the river past St. Michael's churchyard, which Burns said he wanted to be his final resting place, and down Mill Hole Brae to a comfortable two-storey stone house. The poet opened the front door and was nearly bowled over by a young boy. "Bobby, slow down, son," said the father as the boy sped out the door.

"That is a lad of uncommon talents," he boasted. "Seven and already reading Shakespeare. And yet I hope he turns out to be a glorious blockhead and so makes his fortune."

In a well-furnished and carpeted front room, I finally met Mrs. Burns—the long-suffering, former Jean Armour—who sat working a flower pattern with a needle and thread. She was heavily pregnant, dark-haired and about 30 and had once been pretty but now looked coarsened by toil and maternity. Four young children prattled around her feet.

"Jean, you have heard me talk many times about John Bruce, my friend from Edinburgh?" asked Burns.

"Of course. Are you well, sir? I heard you might stop by, and I've a barrel of oysters cooking that a kind country gentleman gave to Mr. Burns."

"That would be very gracious, Mrs. Burns. You have some bonny children there. This young miss, in particular. She's so fair, yet you and Mr. Burns are both so dark. Who does she get that blond hair from?"

There was a long silence as Burns examined the ceiling, and I realized with horror my mistake.

"Well sir, it wouldn't be me. Our rovin' Robin should have had two wives," chuckled Jean before taking the children with her into the kitchen.

When she had gone, Burns turned to me with his head in one hand. "I'll earn a scolding for that, John. Did I not tell you we had taken in the daughter of the barmaid from the Globe, Ann Park?"

"You probably did, but I must confess I'm losing track of all your offspring. But I'm guessing that would be Anna with the golden locks that you rhymed about."

"The very same. It was, I think, my best attempt at a love song. And I've since crafted what I think is a fine anthem to equality that has two or three pretty good prose thoughts inverted into rhyme. It's set to the lively Scots reel, For a' That an' a' That, but I'll spare you the musical rendition."

He walked to a small desk, withdrew some papers and handed them to me. "Tell me what you think of the sentiments, since I'm anxious they may be too radical for these nervous times," he said.

I read the scratchings he'd made and realized I was privileged to be reading a work that was as exceptional as the man who wrote it—a prayer of optimism for a better world that has been read around the globe in the years since it was published.

I read aloud the final stanza:

"For a' that, an' a' that,
It's coming yet for a' that,
That man to man, the world o'er
Shall brothers be for a' that."

"Bravo. It is radical but not meanly so," I said sincerely. "Surely none can take you to task for such noble aspirations?"

He raised his hands in apparent submission. "Well,

the agents of malice and misrepresentation are abroad and are apt to label your humble bard with slanderous falsehoods. Still, I think your point is well made, and I will continue to polish the piece before it sees the light of day."

A tear nearly came to my eye as I nodded my agreement. The new work may not have been sensible or shrewd, coming from a man who relied on a government at war with the revolutionary forces of liberty and equality for his daily bread. Yet it showed the man's creative flame was still alight, even if he had sunk into an obscure existence and was afflicted by failing health.

Jean reappeared and ushered us into the dining room where we enjoyed a meal of fresh country produce. Burns apparently still had friends who supplied him with game and seafood. After dinner the poet walked me back to my lodgings.

"You've never felt the tug of matrimony yet, John?"

"Not thus far, although there have been some near scrapes since you left Edinburgh. Would you ward me off it?"

"Not in so many words. You'll recall that when I pledged myself to Jean over Clarinda, it was in pursuit of a stability that always seemed just out of reach. I have grasped that and cherish it. But in that single-minded chase, I let slip certain other desirable properties."

"Such as?"

He stopped in thought. "Sensuality, passion—and the adventure of houghmagandie," by which he meant fornication, a subject of which he had some gentle understanding. "Perhaps, too, independence and enlightened discourse," he added.

Then he continued, brighter. "Still, there's nothing like it for setting a man's face to the afterlife. Either the delicious morsels of happiness he enjoys in the conjugal yoke give him a longing for the feasts above, or he is a poor husband who wishes to go straight to Hell since it could be no worse." He laughed at his own wit, and I laughed with him since there was no one on earth who was better company than Robert Burns when the mood took him.

The next morning I was preparing to ride north to see one of my law clients in Kilmarnock, before heading back to Edinburgh, when Burns called by and suggested he accompany me part of the way. We crossed the River Nith and rode up its west bank in silence, the blue devils apparently having the poet in their grip once more.

He broke the silence. "My apologies for being in Decemberish humour, as gloomy and sullen as even the deity of dullness could wish for."

"What ails you?" I asked.

"Yourself sir, I think. Your presence brings back so many memories of times when I made decisions that have brought me to my present predicament. And do you know where I am now or soon will be? Raiding haberdashers throughout the town in the search of French gloves, which are contraband goods and expressly prohibited by the laws of this wisely governed realm of ours.

"And after that cursed business, I will be kept employed with my pen in the account books for several days. Fine employment for a poet's pen," he spat in exasperation.

We rode in silence until he proposed he leave me at

Ellisland, the farm he used to work, about five miles outside the town. "The poor wretch who took over the lease of this worn out patch of rock and dust doesn't mind me wandering up and down the banks of the Nith," he said.

We came up a road past a couple of stony fields overrun with rabbits.

On the bank of the river sat a squat farm house and several outhouses. We tethered the horses and walked past flowering hawthorns alongside the river.

"This is where I had the mind for Tam O'Shanter," said the poet, recalling his fine narrative poem. "It was the only decent crop Ellisland ever produced when I farmed here. I'm sure it was me the Hebrew sage prophesized when he foretold, 'And behold, on whatsoever this man doth set his heart, it shall not prosper.'"

It always nagged me that Burns could have been the author of his own deliverance, if only he had been willing to bring together all his fugitive pieces and publish them under another subscription.

"By your own admission, Tam O'Shanter has a polish you may never excel. Yet you handed over a masterpiece gratis for publication by someone else," I said.

He looked at me as if schooling a child. "I'm sure that would be the soundest course for a man of business. But my bardship is a force as natural as the trout swimming in that river. It can't be bought or sold. I am a mighty tax-gatherer before the Lord in order that I might live and rhyme and fix my children on as broad and independent a basis as possible."

"But it's an ignominy that Scotland's bard works as a gauger," I protested.

"Maybe so. But while my present lot may be short of amusement, I pray that it may never be worse."

So there it was. The poet scattered his rhymes like alms while he was condemned to gallop around the countryside collecting back taxes for the princely sum of £50 a year.

As we rode back to the Kilmarnock road where we were to part ways, I reflected that the esteem in which I held him had been restored by his streak of stubbornness, one that refused to bend to circumstance but deeply held a sense of obligation to paint the life he witnessed in all its colours, and to do so with wit and sentiment, regardless of convention.

My faith in him had suffered crises in the past, but by the time we had said our goodbyes, I was once more sitting at the foot of Mount Parnassus, the home of the Muses, gazing up in admiration at the irreducible figure at its summit. While we mortals could only see celestial slivers and crescents, immortal poets could see the whole of the moon.

We both dismounted, and Burns gripped me tightly. "Adieu, my dear Bruce. Sometimes when I am weak as a woman's tear, I fear the worst. But I am tranquil—life is no great blessing. My warmest wishes and prayers to you. And to my Clarinda. Tell her of my most ardent wish for her happiness."

With that he mounted his mare, leaving me weeping like an infant. It was the last I ever saw of him.

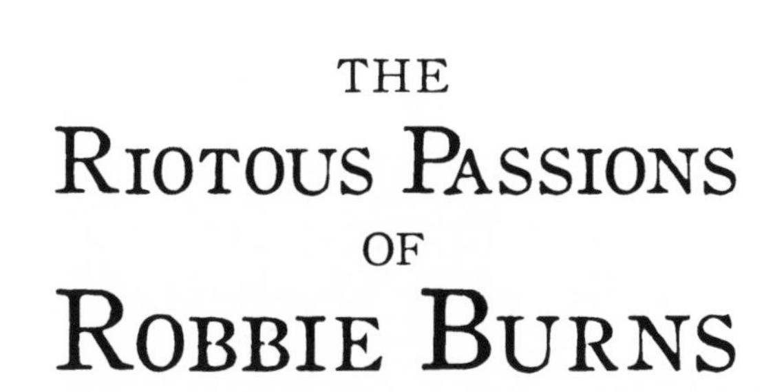

THE

Riotous Passions of Robbie Burns

THE

CAST OF CHARACTERS AND LOCALES

Mrs. Agnes McLehose
(Clarinda)

Robert Burns

Jean Armour

Deacon William Brodie

Crochallan Fencibles

William Smellie

THE

MERRY

MUSES

OF

CALEDONIA;

A COLLECTION OF

FAVOURITE SCOTS SONGS,

Ancient and Modern;

SELECTED FOR USE OF THE

CROCHALLAN FENCIBLES.

Say, Puritan, can it be wrong,
To drefs plain truth in witty fong?
What honeft Nature fays, we fhould do;
What every lady does,--or would do.

PRINTED IN THE YEAR

1799.

CROCHALLAN FENCIBLES

William Dunbar

Charles Hay

Some Figures of the

Adam Smith

Dugald Stewart

SCOTTISH ENLIGHTENMENT

David Hume

Adam Ferguson

Publicans and Publishers

John Dowie — William Creech

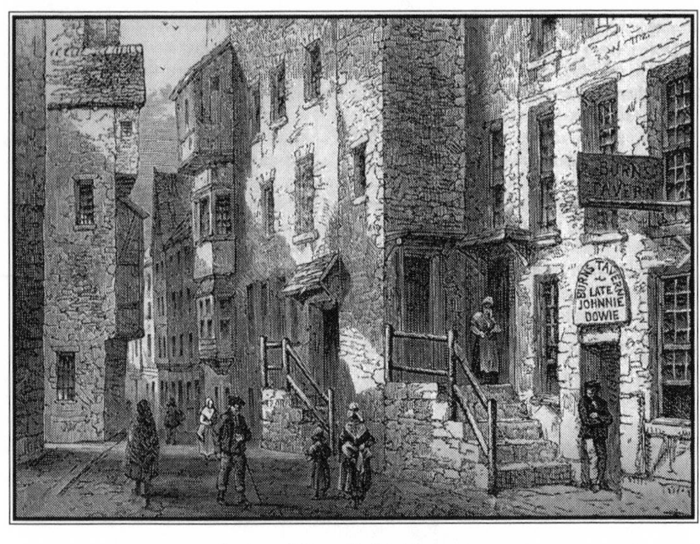

John Dowie's Tavern

EDINBURGH

Edinburgh during the Scottish Enlightenment

Lawnmarket, Robbie Burns' neighbourhood.

The Jolly Beggars

THE END

About the Author

John Ivison is a Scots-Canadian author and journalist. He is a native of Dumfries, where Robert Burns lived, died and is buried.

In a 30-year career in newspapers, Ivison has worked at the *Scotsman*, *Scotland on Sunday* and Canada's *National Post*. In 2019, he published *Trudeau: The Education of a Prime Minister*, the first major biography of Canada's 23rd prime minister, Justin Trudeau.

He is married to Canadian diplomat, Dana Cryderman, and has three children – James, Fiona and William. He lives in Chelsea, Quebec.

Manufactured by Amazon.ca
Bolton, ON